Elizabeth's Hope

A More Perfect Union Series Novella

Betty Bolté

This is a work of fiction. Names, characters, places, and incidents are a product of the author's imagination. Locales and public names are sometimes used for atmospheric purposes. Any resemblance to actual people, living or dead, or to businesses, companies, events, institutions, or locales is completely coincidental.

Betty Bolté
P.O. Box 33
Taft, TN 38488
http://www.bettybolte.com

ALSO BY BETTY BOLTÉ

A MORE PERFECT UNION SERIES
Elizabeth's Hope
Emily's Vow
Amy's Choice
Samantha's Secret
Evelyn's Promise

SECRETS OF ROSEVILLE SERIES
Undying Love
Haunted Melody
The Touchstone of Raven Hollow

Hometown Heroines
True Stories of Bravery, Daring, and Adventure

Chapter 1

Charles Town, South Carolina – April 1780

The familiar silver box reflected the muted sunshine flowing into the parlor as Elizabeth Sullivan angled the rectangular object this way and that in her hands. A gift from the one man she could envision spending her life with, it contained the remembrances of his courtship. Trinkets, really—the note he'd sent asking to court her, a smooth swirly stone picked up on a walk along the beach, even a silver coin he jokingly presented to her as payment for a clandestine, daring kiss—that each held a memory of a shared moment over the past years. But now everything had changed, and their future together had become clouded and doubtful. She set the box aside and rose to move to the front window. She pulled back the drape and studied the distressing view of her beloved city.

Enemy ships of war crowded the harbor; their masts sharp against the eastern sky. Loyalist troops had joined with the British officers outside the city, ready to strike. Elizabeth turned away from the pane of glass and paced the parlor floor, fear simmering in her chest at the recollection of the horrific sight and the knowledge of the impending attack. The sensation was unsettling. Her normally optimistic, buoyant nature felt deadened and heavy. She longed for her father to return from his errand with news. Any news. When would they attack? Would the city leaders capitulate? Then what would happen?

"Emily? Where are you?" She walked through the downstairs rooms, her leather shoes slapping the wood floors, long skirts rustling in her haste. "I cannot tolerate the waiting and worrying."

Emily strode into view, emerging from the dining room. "We must remain strong. Father will come home when he can."

"The constant shooting is wearing on my patience." Elizabeth folded her arms around her waist. "What if he is hurt?"

"We must stay calm, Elizabeth. It is not like you

to be so worried." Emily hurried to her twin sister and embraced her. "Our brave men will protect us from the enemy."

They would certainly try, but the odds were against them. Elizabeth shook her head and stepped away from Emily. "We're running out of food in town and Father said the soldiers are nearly out of ammunition."

Emily blanched and widened her eyes. "I had not heard that news. What will we do?"

The front door opened with a rush of cool air wafting down the hall and then thumped closed. Elizabeth rushed from the parlor to the passage, abruptly halting in the center of the main hall. Joshua Sullivan handed his long black cloak to his manservant and then strode toward his daughters. The scents of the outdoors drifted past her nose. The powerful man stopped before her, his expression serious.

"Father, what news?" Elizabeth clasped her hands together, gripping so hard her fingers ached.

"Our General Benjamin Lincoln sent terms for the surrender of the town to the enemy, Sir Henry Clinton—"

Elizabeth gasped and flung her hands wide. "What? Oh, pray tell me that is not so!"

Father slowly nodded and brought her to him, wrapping his strong arms around her shoulders. "Clinton, as the British Commander-in-Chief, refused to accept certain of the terms, so we are still free."

"You sound as though it is only a matter of time before we will be occupied." Emily moved within the circle to join the embrace.

"Indeed. The city cannot withstand the deprivations much longer." Father squeezed one last time and then dropped his arms to his sides. "We're reduced to firing bits of iron and axes and even broken bottles. All while the men are only given some coffee, sugar, and a few ounces of meat to survive on."

Elizabeth folded her arms across her chest as she studied her father's countenance. Worry had etched lines between his eyes and pinched his expressive mouth. "What will we do when the British take over?"

"I have been thinking about that." He glanced between Elizabeth and Emily. "I want you to go to the Abernathy plantation. Your Uncle Richard and Aunt Lucille are far enough from town not to be in immediate danger from the invasion. They also have many strong hands who can help protect you both."

Elizabeth shook her head before he'd finished speaking. Since her mother had died giving birth to her and Emily, her father had left the household management to her aunt. Then, when Elizabeth and her sister had become old enough, they'd assumed those duties. Thus he'd never had to handle the daily running of the place. "I'll not leave you here alone. You need us to manage the household."

"I'll cope. You need not fear on my behalf."

"I realize other women have left for the back-country, but we do not wish to abandon our home," Emily spoke up, eyes intent upon their father. "I will not run from the enemy."

He studied them both, looking from one obdurate face to the other. Then he sighed and dropped his shoulders in defeat. "Very well, but we have to find out what rules Clinton intends to impose upon any who remain."

"We will do what we must to survive, Father." Elizabeth smoothed the homespun skirts of her last decent dress. "We're Americans."

A knock on the door drew their attention to the front and the street beyond. Solomon appeared from the rear of the house to hurry past them to answer the summons. She noted the set of his mouth and the concern in his brown eyes as he strode past. His white shirt and dark pants had seen much wear, but with no means to replace them, they'd have to do. She could not provide better attire for the slaves, let alone for her and Emily. She wanted to keep up appearances as they always had, but times were difficult, and with the Britons encircling the town, supplies could not reach the trapped inhabitants.

When Solomon pulled the door inward, Elizabeth's heart raced with pleasure to espy Jedediah Thomson filling the opening. Tall, broad of shoulder, his long dark gray cloak brushed the calves of his tall, black boots. A black beaver tricorne topped his chocolate brown hair with strands of gold and red enlivening the color. He smiled at her with a dip of his head and then addressed Joshua.

"I trust we're not interrupting?" Jedediah accepted the silent invitation by Solomon to enter the house. "We've come to bid you farewell for a time."

Behind him, his older brother, Frank, stepped into the cool passageway. Similar in build, Frank differed in having blond hair pulled neatly into a queue beneath his tricorne. He appeared strong and capable in his buff breeches with tall boots, and a white hunting shirt gracing his broad shoulders. Solomon pushed the door closed and then took up a position nearby to be ready if needed. His medium brown skin glistened with sweat despite the cool spring air, the tension of the times reflecting in every person. Elizabeth gave him a quick reassuring smile and then turned her attention to Jedediah.

"Where are you going?" She didn't want him to leave. Ever since her father had introduced her and Emily to the brothers, she'd felt a connection to them, but Jedediah in particular.

Jedediah looked at Frank and then Joshua before regarding her. "Before the enemy takes the town, we must rejoin our unit so we can continue to fight. That's all you really need to know, for your safety."

"What of your house?" Emily frowned as she turned to Jedediah. "And your printing shop?"

"I'm afraid they are a sacrifice I must make." A pained expression flitted across Jedediah's face. "I'd be surprised if they are not invaded by the Britons after we depart."

Frank cleared his throat and then slowly shook his head. "There's nothing to be done. We must get away while there are still holes in the enemy's circle of armed soldiers around the town."

Joshua folded his arms over his intimidating chest. "I'm not giving them my home and business. I'll stay and do what I must to ensure they are not lost. Even foreswear any oath they demand of me. I'll continue to help the Americans, if secretly. But I'm not as young and strong as you two. Fare thee both well and stay the course."

Jedediah nodded in understanding of the directive. "We fully intend to do all in our power to recover the city from their despicable control at the earliest opportunity."

Elizabeth caught Jedediah's eye. "I know you will keep to our efforts for freedom from British rule."

His gaze sharpened as he inclined his head in acknowledgment of her charge. "Elizabeth, I solemnly vow to hold to my duty to defend our state and our country." He hesitated, his expression softening from stern belief to a silent plea. "Will you grant me a moment in private?"

Elizabeth looked at her father with a raised brow. "Father?"

Joshua glanced at her and Jedediah and then nodded. "Be quick about it. I'll not have any questions regarding your reputation getting about town."

"Come into the parlor, Jedediah." She spun and strode into the room she'd occupied before his arrival, all the while wondering what urgent discourse he desired.

A quick perusal of the room proved it was in order. A fire in the fireplace warded off the spring chill. An arrangement of cut flowers from the garden provided a sense of naturalness to the harshly different reality the town faced. Occupied? She shivered at the thought. She walked to a chair by the fireplace and held onto it to steady herself.

Jedediah softly closed the door behind him and then turned to face her, lingering by the door for several moments. Finally, he sauntered to her and took her hands in his, drawing her away from the chair to stand before him.

"I will miss you, Elizabeth." He searched her

face, as if committing to memory each of her features. "Do as your father instructs and be safe."

She smiled, words failing her for several moments. She swallowed concern as she searched his countenance. "You as well, Jedediah. I pray you'll succeed in ultimately freeing us from this oppression."

She studied his face much as he had done to her. Would she ever see him again? Her heart thudded in her ears as she noted his striking blue eyes intent upon her. She and Jedediah had grown close over the time they'd known each other. She thought of the frequent appearance of both the men at the family dinner table of an afternoon, engaging in both happy banter and good-natured debates. The horseback rides she and her sister and the brothers had once enjoyed in the countryside on a pleasant morning. Walks along the Cooper, talking about whatever came to mind. She harbored some hope that one day he would ask for her hand in marriage, but the timing did not seem right with the war dragging on. With the arrival of the British fleet, the thought of marriage had been subsumed by far more frightening concerns.

His eyes focused on hers and then moved to her mouth. She moistened her lips by pressing them together and then relaxing them. His gaze flashed to her eyes and then focused on her mouth again. Slowly he pulled her closer, his head ever so gradually bringing his mouth into proximity with hers. Giving her time to stop his advance. Giving her control of the unexpected and inappropriate kiss he obviously intended bestowing upon her. Despite knowing she should pull away, she leaned forward and closed the distance, pressing her lips to his.

Contact shot a charge of sensation throughout her trembling frame. The delicious desire spread and warmed her body. The forbidden pleasure only served to increase her reaction much like adding logs to the fire. She broke one hand free from his clasp and wound her arm around his neck to draw him closer, ever closer, until their bodies pressed together. After several moments, reality crashed upon her and she broke off the buss, pushing gently against his chest to give herself a moment to restore her composure.

"Elizabeth…" He searched her countenance as he drew in a long breath and released it on a sigh. "I must go."

She inhaled a deep breath as well and slowly let it go. Despair and worry danced in her chest, making her hands tremble all the more. "I understand."

"Do you?" He frowned, clouding the clearness of his eyes. "If not for my pledge to our government to serve, I could easily have remained here, with you."

She nodded and dropped her hands to clasp in front of her skirts. "You must honor your word and fight for our independence. That's your most urgent duty, and I know you will do what is right."

"I will. I also will come back to you as soon as I can." Jedediah stepped away and held out one hand. "Come. I want to say farewell to your father and sister and our time to escape grows short."

So much she could say in response, but every sentiment paled in comparison to what was about to transpire. Better to remain mute and acquiesce. She placed her trembling hand in his, relishing the warmth and strength of his fingers closing over hers. Silently, she permitted him to lead her from the room knowing he carried her heart with him to the front lines.

Chapter 2

Charles Town, South Carolina – May 1780

Why did nothing go as desired? Jedediah rode his horse alongside Frank, walking in the shadows of the forest to avoid detection by the roaming bands of loyalist soldiers. General Gates's forces also roamed, so catching up to the other men had proven more challenging than the brothers had anticipated when they snuck out of Charles Town.

An abrupt rustle behind him had him swinging around in the saddle, his right hand gripping his pistol. Three wild turkeys strutted among the bushes, pecking at the ground. He sighed and turned to face forward.

"Watch out for those loyalist turkeys." Frank chuckled as he steered his mount around a fallen tree. "Relax, we're almost caught up to the others."

"I'll relax when we have rejoined the army." He followed Frank's lead, as he usually did.

His older brother approached life and its challenges with self-assurance and equanimity such as Jedediah had never been able to copy. He'd tried but failed in that endeavor. He wanted to school his emotions so he didn't experience such highs and lows in his day-to-day world. Yet his desires fueled his volatile nature.

The biggest desire he possessed was to choose a wife and start his family before he was too old. After all, he was in his mid-twenties already. What with the war dragging on, though, that desire had been put aside. He'd enlisted to serve the militia until autumn next. When he'd made the commitment he had not anticipated that the war would last that long. He'd hoped an end neared and thus the agreement would be truncated. However, with the British besieging the city, the fighting appeared to stretch far into the future. A life-time.

"Have you considered what the British invasion of our city means for the residents?" Jedediah clucked to his horse and jogged up to ride beside Frank as they worked their way around a meadow dotted with wildflowers.

"Captain Sullivan believes the Britons will require the people to comply with the commandant's restrictions and likely have the men swear allegiance and fealty to King George III."

"Will the captain sign such an oath?" Jedediah considered the burly, brusque man, and recalled his depth of belief in the American cause. He even surreptitiously engaged in privateering with his own ships to the benefit of the new American government. "Is he capable of such deception?"

Frank glanced at him and a slow, secretive smile slipped onto his lips. "He's a survivor. He'll do what he must to ensure that he and his family, his property, and livelihood continue."

"As we must." Jedediah perused the rolling countryside before them. "I trust he will ensure the safety of the girls, though I truly wish we did not have to leave them within the city."

Frank turned to peer at him, halting his horse. "You have feelings for Miss Elizabeth, do you not?"

Jedediah reined in his horse and studied his brother's jocular countenance. Elizabeth's face appeared in his memory, as though she stood in front of him instead. Her beautiful blue eyes with silver flecks. Her long blond tresses caught up in an elaborate style with curls dancing about her jaw. Her alabaster complexion with the slight flush of pleasure when she greeted him. Lovely and intelligent, well read and capable of holding a lively, interesting conversation. He enjoyed her company and longed to keep his promise to return to her. He relived their shared kiss and the touch of her hands in his. He could envision her making a good mate and mother. Feelings, though? That was an entirely different question.

"She is a lovely woman who will make someone a fine life companion." He rested his hands on the pommel of his saddle as he regarded the mirthful grin and laughing eyes staring at him. "What are you smirking about?"

"One of these days the truth will hit you in the heart." Frank shook his head and reined his horse to the right, to continue on their way. "For now, we must pick up the pace or we'll never catch up."

Jedediah urged his gelding into a trot to match his brother's pace, all the while pondering what he meant by the truth. He let the matter drop as they briskly splashed across a creek and then entered the verge of a deep woods. The shadows mingled about them as they hurried on along the pine needle covered trail between the massive trunks of the ancient forest, with luck gaining ground on the ever restless troops as the patriots searched out pockets of loyalists in the back-country. Slowly the American General Gates was trying to reclaim command of the region, tightening a noose around the British commander's neck.

They trotted up a slight rise, sunlight shooting rays illuminating swirling clouds of insects, and then started down a sharper slope toward a river he could hear in the distance. Suddenly, two men in loyalist dress jumped out from behind trees flanking the trail, their rifles aimed at the brothers. Frank yanked on the reins, causing his horse to rear. Jedediah halted beside him, his horse prancing nervously, scattering pine needles into the underbrush.

"Who goes there?" The bearded man glared at Jedediah, shaggy brows drawn together beneath a drooping Monmouth cap.

Frank tossed a look at Jedediah, a slight tilt of his head indicating for him to follow his lead. "We're just a couple of soldiers on our way to rejoin our unit."

"Yeah? And what unit might that be?" The other man aimed his weapon at Frank, his scowl revealing his distrust.

Frank shot another look at Jedediah and then gathered his reins as he kept his nervous horse moving beneath him. Jedediah followed Frank's movements, shortening his reins in preparation for whatever plan to avoid capture his brother had settled upon. When Frank lifted his legs from the sides of his horse ready to kick him on,

Jedediah did the same. Frank yelled and sent his horse into the man closest to him, knocking him to the ground, as Jedediah aimed for the second man. The bearded man shouted a curse as he scrabbled sideways behind the tree. He still possessed his gun, so Jedediah kicked his horse into a gallop to chase after Frank between the trees. A shot rang out, and a bullet whizzed past him and *thunked* into a pine, sending bits of bark flying into the air. Jedediah crouched lower and rode for his life. Another shot, then another, but no more bullets reached near him as he increased the distance between the loyalist soldiers and himself. He glanced back as his horse burst into a clearing. They weren't being followed at least.

Frank cantered around the edge of the open field until he found a copse of fully leafed bushes and trees they could hide in to catch their breath and give their heaving horses a break.

"Brazen plan of escape." Jedediah rested his hands on his thighs, the reins long and loose to let his horse graze. "Which almost got us shot."

"It worked." Frank grinned at him, as casual and calm as if he were sitting at home under a shade tree instead of hiding out from their attackers. "That is the important result."

Jedediah shook his head slowly, keeping a watchful eye out for any activity. "That and we made up some time with that gallop. Let's keep going."

"Good idea." Frank urged his horse into a trot and led the way out into the open.

Jedediah was content to let his brother lead, even if his actions could at times be considered reckless. Frank held their safety as his highest priority, so Jedediah trusted him implicitly. They rode along, chatting about this and that, or lapsing into a companionable silence, covering as much distance as they could.

Finally, after what seemed like hours, Frank halted his horse and motioned with one hand. "Look, there's an army camp ahead."

Reining in beside him, Jedediah followed the direction of his pointing finger. He could see columns of smoke rising into the bright blue sky from a group of white tents scattered across a meadow. A cluster of horses were picketed to one side under the cool shade of several magnolias and oaks.

"Is it Gates?" Jedediah peered at the men and women milling about the tents and tending the fires. "Can you tell from this distance?"

Frank nodded with a smile stretching on his face. "Yes, from the flag flying near that largest of tents. It's General Gates's headquarters I'm thinking."

Jedediah looked more closely at the

encampment and finally spotted the flag. Red and white stripes, with a blue union and white stars. Relief flooded his chest.

"Let's go." He nudged his horse into a trot then a canter.

Frank matched his pace as they approached the end of their perilous journey. Not that the peril ended by arriving at the army camp. No, in truth, it was just beginning.

Chapter 3

Charles Town, South Carolina – September 1780

Who could she trust? That was the question plaguing Elizabeth as she and Emily strolled along King Street to the market, accompanied by Solomon and Jasmine to help and protect the ladies. The occupation of the town after the leaders had capitulated as expected stretched on, now into its fourth month, and the effects were definitely being felt by everyone. She could only hope to find food they could afford to purchase. Limited quantities of everything led to exorbitant prices. The last time they'd made the futile trip the cost of a pumpkin exceeded the amount of coin money they had on hand. Paper money proved worthless to the British and loyalist merchants. Without more specie, how would they survive?

"Mayhap the fish will suffice to tide us over until Father can bring in more victuals on his ships." She acknowledged a passing woman, Mrs. Darlene Walters, dressed in black, mourning the occupation as much as she and Emily did even though they were forced to act loyal to the crown. That was one way to know who was truly a patriot. Those who declared loyalty yet remained a patriot at heart were more difficult to detect. Like her father. "Morning, Mrs. Walters."

"Good morning to you, Elizabeth. Emily." Mrs. Walters tilted her head, her brown hair peeking out from beneath her black bonnet. "Will I see you at the sewing circle this afternoon?"

"Yes, ma'am, we will be there." Elizabeth smiled at her, as they paused to chat. "Our aunt is happy to host such a worth while gathering."

The patriotic ladies in town met once or twice a week to spin, weave, and sew fabric into shirts and pants for the soldiers fighting for the American cause. Flax and hemp grew in the gardens and then the plants were harvested and stored until needed to provide the raw materials. The finished items were smuggled out of town using various means, including townspeople leaving the confines under the protection of a pass given to loyalists. Which they could only acquire thanks to the efforts of those like her father who walked a perilous path indeed.

"Emily, will you be able to bring your loom? I know how cumbersome it must be to move it."

"Yes, ma'am, I'll be sure it's there and ready to use." Emily dipped her head in acknowledgment. "It won't be any trouble at all."

Not with the two strong slaves, Solomon and Richard, to handle the heavy equipment and Jasmine to carry the spools and skeins needed. Elizabeth regarded Emily for a short while as she conversed with the other woman. Elizabeth ensured the servants had decent apparel and footwear, both so they were comfortable and so they presented an acceptable appearance. Her sister could be oblivious to the needs and wants of their servants upon occasion but not on purpose. Emily tried to understand the necessities of others but then became wrapped up in her thoughts. Thoughts she committed to paper and squirreled away. What did she intend to do with all her writings? The answer to that question also worried Elizabeth as ladies were strongly discouraged from writing let alone publishing their scribblings. To do so was beneath Emily's station as the daughter of an esteemed merchant and would mar her reputation.

"Magnificent. I shall see you later." Mrs. Walters gave a weak smile and then sauntered away.

"She's quite supportive of our clandestine and subversive activities." Emily threw a glance over her shoulder at the departing figure and then glanced at Elizabeth. "I like her."

Chuckling, Elizabeth smiled at her sister. "Me, too. Let's not talk too boldly about those efforts. Not in public."

Emily cast a fearful look about the area. "What are we to do, Elizabeth?"

"Stay the course. Keep unto ourselves and try to behave as if we support the loyalist cause." She pinned her sister with a look. "We must endure until the war is over."

"Do you think our brothers will survive, wherever they are?" Emily returned the serious regard. "Or that they'll fight alongside Frank and Jedediah?"

"I do not know. Father received a missive from our brothers this morning, but it did not contain such specifics."

"He showed me the letter, but I had hoped his contacts might yield more intelligence than what they'd written." Emily sighed, a long heart-rending sound. "I miss them so. Have you received any more letters from the Thomson brothers?"

"Not since Jedediah wrote last month to let me know they were safe after the horrendous defeat at Camden." She'd only received it through the kindness of one of his compatriots who smuggled it into town. Relief washed through her, but at the same moment concern as to Jedediah and Frank's ability to remain alive with all the conflicts swelled inside. "He expects a new general to assume command later this year, after that cowardly Gates fled the battlefield in disgrace."

"I pray they will all come home to us without injury." Emily frowned at Elizabeth, worry evident in her blue eyes. "It's so hard to simply carry on and not be able to do more for our cause."

"That is what we need to do for our men, Emily. Carry on and tend the household, so they have a home to return to." Elizabeth shrugged lightly, a quick lift and fall of her slender shoulders. "We need to focus on the things we can take care of and not fill our heads with worries over things we cannot control."

"I find that difficult. I dread attending church with that British-supplied loyalist preacher spouting nonsense." Emily clutched her soft purse in both hands, mangling the fabric. "I do not believe the terrible views of our men's actions that he pushes down our throats."

"We're not required to believe what he says, Emily." She did not enjoy the sermons and prayers any more than her twin. At least their father did not require them to attend every week. "I pity the school children who must listen to the blathering of the loyalist teachers every day."

Emily shook her curls as they turned toward the market. "That would be intolerable."

They strode into the cluster of makeshift tables holding the various foods and wares offered for sale. Chatter vied with the cries of the gulls and babies, the hawking of vegetables and meats as well as candles and baskets. The aromas of hot roasted peanuts and cool bayberry filled the crisp fall air. A gentleman sauntered along the sandy street leading his water spaniel, a good-size dog with curly caramel colored hair, his pink tongue lolling. A lady browsed the offerings, her pet monkey dressed in a tiny British uniform perched on her shoulder. A typical day in some ways, but with the ominous shadow of the enemy blanketing the discourse and exchanges. Wandering along, she stopped in front of the eager fish monger.

"How fresh are the oysters?" She indicated the bowl filled with the gray-shelled mollusks.

"Caught this morning." He lifted the shallow bowl to angle the contents for best viewing. "How many do you want?"

She eyed him with one brow lifted. "How much are you asking?"

He quoted a price that had her lifting both brows. She haggled with him until the eagerness in his eyes dimmed. After a few more offers from either side, they settled on a price for two dozen.

As he wrapped her purchase, she sighed. They needed to eat, but where would she find the money to buy new shoes for herself let alone for her sister? Until she could do so, her faithful maid Jasmine must continue to wear the worn out ones she'd been putting up with for months. Elizabeth's heart hurt at not being able to maintain the standards they had always aimed to achieve. How they dressed and presented themselves bespoke their class without words, a station in life her father had labored to achieve.

Until the war ended, the soaring costs and scarcity of everything would surely continue to get worse. Right along with the deprivations and deceptions necessary to survive as best they could. She let her gaze drift around the market square, noting the British soldiers standing in clusters, watching the people like hungry birds of prey. Beady eyes following their every move. Waiting for any careless patriots to reveal themselves so they could pounce and exact their vengeance for placing them in such a precarious position.

"Come, Emily, we should go home now that all our money has been spent on supper." She focused on the concern in her sister's eyes. "Then we must finish our daily tasks before we go to Aunt Lucille's."

Emily bobbed her head as she fell into step beside Elizabeth. "Indeed. If I can do nothing else, then at least I can provide comfort to those fighting on our behalf. And against our enemy."

"Do you think we should continue with our plans for the yearly Allhallows Eve dinner next month? And our other traditions?" She glanced at Emily and then at the street ahead as they walked home. "The British have their balls and parties which we shall not attend, but is it wise to maintain our usual festivities?"

"I believe it is important to have something to hold as a candle against the black night of this occupation." Emily shifted the basket of oysters she carried. "We should make some plans for the event. Including convincing Father to tell a story."

"We should request Cousin Amy to regale us with one of her wonderful tales." She smiled, recalling the many ghastly and spooky stories their cousin had invented in years past. "She's a born storyteller with a gift of a fine imagination."

"I fear her talents may lead her astray, but you're correct that she can create fine stories." Emily stepped to one side to let another couple pass. Resuming her pace, she glanced at Elizabeth. "She'll need a distraction this year, since Benjamin Hanson also fled the town. At least the Thomson brothers bade us farewell."

"Where did Benjamin go? Do you know?" Elizabeth retied her bonnet after a gust of wind lifted it.

"No one knows. He left without a word." Gripping the basket with both hands, Emily looked at Elizabeth. "Here I thought he cared for her. So she will need something else to occupy her thoughts."

"Then it's settled. We'll celebrate Allhallows, then the advent of the winter holidays with Christmas and the conclusion of them with Twelfth Night in January." Happy occasions to look forward to during the long, dark days of the winter as well as of the occupation.

Although happy must be relative given the situation. Little food or drink. Stifled expression of thoughts. The news controlled by the enemy so that the patriots were deprived of any morale-boosting information regarding the American cause of independence. But worst of all, their men in danger and regular life curtailed. All she wanted was for the war to end and for all the men to return to their families. Most importantly, for Jedediah to return to her.

Chapter 4

Charlotte, North Carolina – December 1780

The winter encampment lived up to its name. Jedediah wanted nothing more than to be home in Charles Town where it was warmer, and it didn't snow. Back in the house he had built with his own hands. A sturdy, two-story abode with its many windows and double piazza. The inlaid mahogany floor supporting the immense table he'd crafted. Home. He shivered inside his thin coat as he rode through the town alongside his brother. The arrival of Major General Nathanael Greene had sparked optimism and lifted the morale of the freezing and ill-clad soldiers going about their day, drilling, scavenging for supplies, but mainly waiting for orders.

"I keep hoping those above us will find a way to win this war." Frank's shoulders jerked in a severe shiver as snowflakes drifted lazily to land on his black cloak. "Then we can look forward to the next day without dread."

"There's no end in sight at the moment, I'm afraid." Jedediah kept his eyes open and aware as they approached General Greene's headquarters near the town square. He didn't expect any loyalists to attack, especially not in such a patriot stronghold, but he would stay alert. The patriot forces residing in the town were preparing to attack the British from their temporary home. *Home.* He glanced at Frank. Should he even mention how his thoughts continually strayed to home? To Elizabeth? After Frank's nudge about his feelings toward the pretty woman, she hadn't left his musings.

They rode for a minute in silence. People of the town went about their daily activities, hurrying through the streets, dodging horses and conveyances of every kind. Dogs trotted about or sniffed along the ground, tracking an intriguing scent. The town had been returned to their hands after the British had abandoned camp months previous. A resulting sense of relief permeated the very air he breathed. He longed for home every moment of every day. Yet his duty remained with his fellow soldiers and to the cause for which they all fought.

"Frank, I must confess to you how much I wish this war would conclude." Jedediah followed Frank as he turned down a side street toward the brick home where Greene had established his headquarters.

Frank reined up, stopping in the lane to wait for Jedediah to join him. "Thinking about a certain lady?"

Jedediah blinked and shook his head. "It's uncanny how you read my thoughts. Yes, as a matter of fact, I have been thinking of her often."

A smile spread on his brother's lips as he nodded. "I thought so. What exactly have your thoughts been with regard to Miss Elizabeth?"

He searched his mind for a way to convey how his heart had been wrestling with his mind over his next moves, much like playing chess with emotions prevailing. "When I have completed my enlistment, I believe I want to marry her and keep her in a fine fashion. I believe we will make each other happy."

"The truth shall see you married." Frank chuckled. "That's a play on words, in case you missed it."

"You're right." Jedediah shifted in the saddle, and his horse stepped forward. He halted him again and then regarded his brother. The allusion to the bible verse put emphasis on his desire to be wed by the minister. "You mentioned before about a truth and only recently did I comprehend your meaning. I desire to be bound to Elizabeth for eternity. She will not only be a fine wife and mother, but a steady companion through hard and easy times."

"Perhaps one day I'll follow your lead." Frank grinned at him, his gray eyes filled with mirth. "I have found Emily to be quite tantalizing and engaging."

"I've noticed your interest in her and applaud the idea of your asking for her hand." Indeed, Jedediah had dragged Frank along with him to the Sullivans for frequent dinners for the express purpose of keeping Emily's agreeable person before Frank. His brother would benefit from having someone look out for his wellbeing and Emily had a good education like his Elizabeth. His? Not yet, but he was going to make that a priority. "I have an idea."

"Should I be worried given that conspiratorial grin you're exhibiting?"

"Probably. What if we surprise the ladies on Twelfth Night for their annual dinner party?" His thoughts were flying as he contemplated the permissions and plans involved in making his wild thought a reality. How would he convince his commander to permit them leave? Sneak into the enemy-held town without being seen? He didn't know, but he'd figure it out. "Then I could ask her father and her at the same time."

"Ask her to marry you?" Frank frowned and shook his head slowly. "You still have months before you're finished with your commitment."

"I'm well aware of my pledge and will maintain it. But I need to know if she'll be waiting for me when September finds me free to pursue my own destiny."

"If you're sure you want to become betrothed…" Frank shrugged as he regarded Jedediah with wide eyes. "I'm willing to accompany you if only for a couple of days. After all, you need someone to have your back."

"With the fighting concluded for the winter, we should be able to obtain a pass to visit our family, but we'll need to find a way to sneak into town without discovery."

"Let me handle that. I'm good at comings and goings that are undetected." He smiled openly at Jedediah. "After all, that is why the general wants me to start spying instead of soldiering."

The sound of horses' hooves approaching at a good pace made Jedediah turn. Three men, all wide-shouldered, brawny, and with matching dark hair, cantered toward them. He peered at them as they drew closer and then saluted, which drew their attention. The lead man raised a hand, and all three slowed to a trot and then stopped by Jedediah and Frank.

"Ethan Sullivan? Is that you?" Jedediah inclined

his head briefly in greeting. "And, of course, Bill and Luke. What brings you all here?"

"Greetings, Jedediah. I'm pleased to see you and Frank both hale and hearty after the battles this year." Ethan, Elizabeth's oldest brother, had a booming voice which drew the attention of passersby. "We've been assigned to serve under Brigadier General Daniel Morgan when he ventures into the back-country to wipe out the loyalist nests."

"I can't wait to ride out there and show them how mistaken they were to side with the British," Bill asserted. "Time for this terrible war to end."

"We were saying the same thing," Frank said, addressing each of the brothers. "Home never sounded so good, especially as the holiday season looms."

The youngest of the Sullivan brothers, Luke, agreed as he calmed his horse with a hand on its withers. "Unfortunately, General Morgan has orders for us to head for the back-country of South Carolina within the next few weeks, so home will not see our faces for some time."

"We have not received our orders yet, but they should come soon." Then they'd figure out if they could indeed slip home for a brief but important visit at the Sullivan home. As long as those orders didn't take them farther afield, they might be able to arrange things to their advantage. "You all take care and return to your family in due course."

Ethan nodded slowly, gathering his reins to continue on their way. "You two, as well."

The three men rode off at a canter, a dust cloud rising to mingle with the flurries.

"Come on, Jedediah; we need to report and find out which of those log huts we'll be sleeping in tonight."

"Lead on." He trotted after his brother, knowing in his heart that he had settled on a path to his future. But how circuitous a path would it be?

Chapter 5

Charles Town, South Carolina – January 5, 1781

The Twelfth Night feast did not live up to its name. Elizabeth had gathered what she could find, which ended up being a paltry assortment of dried fruits, nuts, and a single apple cake to be divided among the guests. Not that there would be many guests either. Tensions in the town ran high. Father had even requested that she and Emily only go outside when necessary. An idea that rankled deep inside her heart. The very idea that she was not free to walk the streets of her own town. Appalling. She sauntered through the house, checking each room to ensure everything was straightened up and ready.

Emily came down the stairs; a pale yellow gown draped over one arm. She paused in the passage, waiting for Elizabeth to stop in front of her. "I need your opinion."

"If it's about your sewing, all I can say is that you're amazing with a needle." Elizabeth fingered the satin, savoring the smooth texture as well as liking the pretty color. "What did you need?"

"I know it's premature, but I had this idea for a dress to wear in the event I should ever marry. Which of course looks doubtful at this late point in my life."

"We're not that old, Em. We're only in our mid-twenties after all. But I see you're serious." Elizabeth chuckled as she crossed her arms over her chest. "What did you need?"

Emily indicated the dress on her arm. "I thought I might add seed pearls in rays from the bodice to the skirts. Do you think that would look pretty or is it too much?"

She cocked her head, trying to imagine the changes to the gown. "I think that would be lovely."

A knock sounded at the door and Jasmine hurried to answer it. Her long, plain brown skirts swished and shushed as she slipped past the sisters with a grin for them. Her dark hair was pulled into a severe bun tied with a bit of green ribbon. Elizabeth returned the smile, knowing the woman had a fondness for them. Jasmine had been a part of their lives since before the war began and had become a trusted confidante.

"Go put your dress away as our guests have begun to arrive." Elizabeth shooed Emily up the stairs with a wave of her hands. "Hurry back, though."

Emily nodded once and trotted up the stairs and out of sight. Elizabeth turned to greet her cousin Amy. Behind her, Aunt Lucille and Uncle Richard stepped into the house, snow flurries rushing in on the breeze. She caught a glimpse of two British soldiers lounging outside before Jasmine snugged the door closed. Since her father had signed the oath of allegiance to the crown, the soldiers had taken to keeping a watch out front of the house so they could partake of their meager offerings whenever it suited them. After all, her father had agreed to support their cause, at least on paper. Shaken by their presence, but determined to hide her reaction, Elizabeth embraced Amy, giving her a quick kiss on the cheek before greeting her aunt and uncle.

"I'm so happy you've arrived. While we don't have a great deal to offer, being with you makes the holidays complete." She motioned to Jasmine to collect their coats and cloaks and then led the way to the dining room where the food was laid out on the table.

"Nobody would expect to have much merrymaking in an occupied city." Richard slowly shook his head as he picked up a nut and popped it into his mouth. "I've been told the British are celebrating their occupation by throwing lavish balls and dinners."

Lucille nodded, then paused, listening. She strode over to the window to peer outside into the dark. She remained motionless for several moments and then glanced over her shoulder at the group. "Did you hear something?"

"Come away from the window, my dear." Richard waved at his wife, beckoning her to return to the center of the room. "If there is someone out there, we do not know their intentions."

"What did you hear?" Elizabeth strode over to join Lucille, looking through the imperfect window pane.

"Voices. Of men. Perhaps more of your guests?" Lucille aimed a querying look at Elizabeth. "Why would they not have come to the front door like decent folk?"

Joshua and Emily strode into the room together, drawing Elizabeth's attention. Her father appeared on edge, his gaze darting from person to person and then settling upon Elizabeth. She hesitated to query him regarding the possibility of someone behind the house, but if there was anything amiss, then he should be informed.

"Father, Aunt Lucille heard some men outside the window. It may simply be some of the hands." She walked over to stand with her father, glancing at Emily's concerned expression. "Will you send someone to check it out, please?"

"Indeed I shall." He spun on one heel and left the room, calling to Solomon as he disappeared.

"While Father investigates, let's have some blackberry wine we managed to hide away for this special occasion." Elizabeth stifled the impulse to follow her parent as she crossed to the sideboard and lifted the cut-glass decanter.

"Sounds like a fine idea." Amy joined her, helping to hand out the filled glasses.

The back door opened, and the sound of booted feet halted Elizabeth in the act of pouring the wine. She turned to stare at the door, her actions mirrored by the others. Male voices, low and urgent, sent a chill down her spine. The door closed, softly, as though to avoid announcing the fact that someone had entered the house. She set down the glass decanter and swallowed hard. Who had her father discovered hiding behind the house?

"Look who I found." Joshua's booming voice startled her, making her jump. "Elizabeth, come here."

When she saw who was behind him, joy swept through her. "Jedediah!"

Jedediah darted around Joshua and hurried to

her, clasping both her hands in his as a huge smile settled onto his lips. "Hello, Elizabeth."

"What are you doing here?" She squeezed his fingers as she searched his expression. Fear warred with the joy at seeing him safe and sound. She noted Frank's arrival in the open door and realized the danger they both faced. If the soldiers out front learned of their presence, they would be arrested. Elizabeth trembled as she gazed into Jedediah's eyes. "You shouldn't be here."

"I told you I'd return to you." He glanced at her father who nodded once, an answering smile on his face. "We do not have long, my sweet. I have something I must ask you."

She waited, seeing him preparing to say something important. Loving the sight of him. The touch of his hands on hers. The memory of his kiss. She smiled at him, encouraging him to speak his mind.

"Elizabeth, I have missed you more than I can say. I have come to realize that I do not wish to live my life without you with me. I've come here, on this very special night, to ask you to give me your hand in marriage."

She blinked as tears pushed for release, one drop sliding slowly along her cheek. She glanced at her father, saw his nod and grin, and then gazed up at Jedediah's serious countenance. She swallowed and nodded.

"Is that a yes?" Jedediah's mouth opened slightly, waiting for her confirmation.

"Yes, Jedediah, I'll marry you." She smiled at him through her tears of joy. "I promise that I'll be a good wife to you and always care for you for as long as I live."

Frank cleared his throat and then clapped, leading the others to join in for a moment or two. "Best tidings on a long and happy life together."

Elizabeth smiled at Frank and then her sister. "Emily, you see, it can happen, even at our advanced age."

Frank looked sharply at Elizabeth, making her chuckle, then turned his eyes to regard Emily's happy expression. He opened his mouth as if to say something and then snapped his lips together. *Curious.*

"Does this mean you two are betrothed?" Emily asked.

Elizabeth smiled, swiping away the tears from her cheeks. "Yes, it does."

"I must complete my commitment to the army first, so we'll need to wait until autumn. Will that suit?"

Anything. As long as she knew he was hers and would come home to her. "I'll wait as long as it takes, Jedediah. I understand how important your word and your duty are to you, and I wouldn't change that about you."

"Thank you. You are one special woman."

Jedediah lowered his head to press his lips to hers. She closed her eyes at the touch and the sweeping sensation spreading through her core. Her family erupted in "huzzas" and clapping.

Jedediah gazed at her, giving her hands a squeeze and then pulled her closer to him. "I love you."

"I love you." Elizabeth's heart filled and then overflowed with happiness. But somehow she could only wonder if love was enough. What more did she desire?

Chapter 6

Charles Town, South Carolina – February 1781

"Elizabeth, a special delivery for you." Emily carried something in her hand as she approached her sister.

"What is it?" Elizabeth waited where she sat knitting a sock to ward off the cold of the winter on her toes. A hunting dog curled up by her feet, lifting his head to blink at the interruption to his nap.

A fire blazed in the large firebox; red, orange, and blue flames licking the sides of the logs piled upon one another. The pops and hisses accompanied the sound of Emily's satin slippers on the wood floor. Elizabeth studied the smiling features on her sister's face as she handed a letter to her, a pink ribbon wrapped around it and tied into a bow.

Elizabeth held the paper, folded neatly to conceal the message inside. She looked up at her sister. "Who do you think it's from?"

"One guess." Emily crossed her arms and grinned. "Is it for Valentine's Day?"

A thrill rushed through her as she slowly tugged on the ribbon to untie the pretty bow. She fingered the smooth material, imagining Jedediah's fingers touching the same ribbon when he attached it to the missive. She gazed at the strip of cloth, wondering at his ability to procure such an item in the middle of a war. Leave it to his ingenuity. Laying the ribbon in her lap, she unfolded the page and quickly read his words. Words that conveyed his longing to be with her, of the determination to succeed in the cause of independence in spite of the severe hardships faced by the men. A frown settled onto her brows as she looked up at Emily.

"He is fine. I'm so relieved." After the news of the frequent skirmishes in the back-country between Morgan's forces and the loyalists, her brothers were at risk. She didn't know where her love might be as he was assigned to Greene's forces, so she prayed for his and Frank's safety constantly. "He says our brothers are also fine, despite the ferocious fighting at Cowpens recently."

"That's wonderful news." Emily sank onto a nearby chair and laid her hands in her lap, fingers interlocked and relaxed. "I worry about them as much as the Thomson brothers."

Elizabeth glanced at the letter from Jedediah, where he'd signed it as from her Valentine, a little heart inscribed next to his signature. She smiled at his declaration of love and then read again the paragraph depicting the horrific fighting their brothers had endured. "Apparently Bill got mixed up in something that upset him, but he survived the battle."

"I do wish this war would end so they could all come home." Emily shook her head and then pinned a serious look on Elizabeth. "I try not to ponder any of them not returning."

"I as well." She folded the page again and laid it and the ribbon on the table at her elbow. Next time she fixed her hair, she'd wear it as he asked and think of him. Though she always thought of Jedediah and the future they'd have together. She picked up her knitting and resumed the steady click clack of the needles, calming the agitation Emily's sentiments had stirred up inside. "We must keep the faith, Em. We will see Jedediah, Frank, and our brothers again."

The front door opened and shut, followed by

heavy footsteps in the passage. Elizabeth glanced at the open door of the parlor as her father filled it. "Good, you're both here."

"What news do you bring, Father?" Elizabeth kept her hands busy as Joshua went to the fireplace and warmed his hands by its heat.

Jasmine entered the room, crossing to stand by Emily's chair. She stood silently, waiting for any instructions. Elizabeth noted the patches on her gown, but had neither money nor fabric for a new one. The clothing the sewing circle made all went to support the troops. The ladies would have to make do. Her preferences must be delayed until such a time when it would be more appropriate. She smiled at Jasmine and then returned her attention to her father.

"Good tidings. Morgan is worrying the British. He's freed areas in Georgia and our state with each triumph. That is why I've come looking for you both." He turned from the fireplace and captured Elizabeth's attention. "Your aunt and uncle intend to return to their plantation to gather supplies from whatever remains there. I want you to go with them before there is a battle to free our fair city from British control. I believe you and your sister will be safer away from town as things currently stand."

"Leave the city? What about you?" She didn't desire to leave the relative calm of the city, even if it was under the enemy's control. Elizabeth espied her father's determination in the set of his jaw.

He waved a hand back and forth, dismissing her concerns. "I'll manage, do not fret. I must stay here to keep my interests operating as best I can under the present situation."

"We've discussed this before. I do not want to abandon you, Father." Emily rose to cross the carpet and stand before him. "You need us to take care of you."

Joshua chuckled and laid both hands on Emily's slim shoulders. "You worry too much about this old bird. I have fended for myself before, my darling daughter."

The knitting needles continued their steady rhythm as Elizabeth considered the possibilities of escaping the confines of the besieged town. Mayhap they'd be able to walk and ride without an armed escort again. Fearful of stray bullets and even more wayward enemy soldiers bent on causing havoc and harm. Outside of the control of the enemy mayhap Jedediah could find a way to visit without the awful fear of capture. That last thought brought a grin to her lips. "Father, would we be permitted to leave?"

He nodded, dropping his hands from Emily's shoulders as he turned to face her. "I can arrange a monthly pass for you to visit and bring in whatever you can from the country. As women, you do not require the same oversight as the men. My oath of loyalty also brings privileges of its own. A happy circumstance indeed."

"But Elizabeth, why would you desire to go?" Emily frowned at her, her hands wringing each other as she gazed at Elizabeth.

In spite of the dismissal of women her father's comment revealed, she was willing to take advantage of the opinion for her own ends. "I think it is a fine idea." She stopped the flying needles in her hands and laid the sewing on top of the loving letter from her betrothed. "We should make haste to put the plan into action."

"Very well." Joshua smiled as he nodded at the girls. "I shall make the arrangements immediately." He strode briskly out of the room and then the front door opened and closed.

"Elizabeth, this is absurd." Emily walked over to look at her sister. "I don't want to go to the plantation. They've all been ransacked and abused over the past months. What purpose might it serve to venture beyond the town's borders?"

Elizabeth held up a finger toward Emily as she glanced at their maid. "Jasmine, we do not need anything at the moment. Why don't you see if you can help Mary in the kitchen?"

"Yes, miss." Jasmine bobbed a curtsy and left the room.

"As to your question, Emily." Elizabeth stood

and regarded her sister with an irrepressible grin. "Because, my dear sweet sister, if we leave this captured city and are in the country, then perchance Jedediah and Frank will be able to visit us."

Emily's brows shot up as understanding settled in her mind. "If they can get permission to do so…"

Elizabeth nodded. "It would be much safer for them to come to the plantation." She gripped Emily's hands in hers. The delight that sprung into her heart made it race with joy. "I so wish to see Jedediah I'd do anything, go anywhere I have to, so that he could come to me. Please, Em."

She waited while Emily considered for several moments the request to journey beyond the town into the wilder countryside for an indefinite period. Out to where the skirmishes continued and random attacks occurred on both sides. Finally, Emily sighed and squeezed Elizabeth's hands.

"I'll start packing. I understand your desire." Emily shook her head slowly, side to side, and then grinned. "I wouldn't mind the chance to see Frank, you know."

"Thank you, Em. You won't regret this." Elizabeth released Emily's hands and gathered up her sewing and Jedediah's letter. She would write to him to inform him of their plan, and then wait and see if he would come to her. If he *could* come to her.

Chapter 7

Abernathy Plantation – February 1781

His horse couldn't traverse the distance between the army encampment and his destination fast enough for his liking. The general had been very clear as to when he must be back in camp. Too soon, to his mind. Jedediah pushed his gelding to reach the Abernathy home to allow time to visit with his love for as long as possible given his short grant of leave from his duties. The troops were resting between skirmishes and battles, recovering their strength and repairing equipment and clothing in preparation for the next one.

He galloped up the carriageway to the impressive manor house and swung from the saddle. Under other circumstances, he'd have taken time to study the building, to appreciate the style and construction. But not today. He heard a hand call out, announcing his arrival. A scrawny black boy ran out to take the reins so Jedediah could hurry up the front steps. The door swung open as he raised a fist to knock, and there she was. Elizabeth. Looking fresh and beautiful as a rose.

"Jedediah!" Elizabeth ran to him, surprising him by throwing herself into his arms.

He clasped her to him, grateful to have her next to him. "Elizabeth, I've missed you so much. I was overjoyed when I received your note."

She broke away, but grabbed his hand and pulled him inside the house. "It's so cold; you must come in and warm yourself."

He let her lead him into a small but warm room off the main passage. The décor suggested it was primarily used for entertaining, with fine wood and marble furniture and painted cloths adorning the floors. Framed portraits of famous personages graced the walls and occupied easels on the sideboard. She ushered him to the couch facing the cheery fireplace and encouraged him to sit before joining him.

"I do not have long with you, my dear." Jedediah held onto her hand, not ready to relinquish their connection. "I must be back at camp by to-morrow evening."

"That's no time at all." She sighed heavily and searched his expression. "Why must you fly away so soon?"

"I'm needed, my love." He pulled her to him and kissed her for several moments. "But I had to come to you when I learned you were within a half-day's ride."

"I'll cherish the time." She kissed him lightly and a smile graced her luscious lips.

"Elizabeth, where are you?" Lucille Abernathy strode into the room and smiled when she saw him sitting beside her niece. "Jedediah, how nice to see you well. What brings you here?"

"Elizabeth told me she is visiting and the General took pity on me to allow me to see my betrothed." He recalled the sly smile on the man's face when he realized the real reason for the request for leave. "So here I am."

"I'll have some tea brought in, and we can all catch up on what has been transpiring." Lucille walked out of the room, calling for her servant to prepare a tray.

Jedediah realized the aunt took proper measures to ensure Elizabeth's reputation would not be marred by her being unchaperoned. Given the way Elizabeth had greeted him, her steps were indeed necessary. Her eager welcome played again in his mind, and he smiled.

While they waited for the arrival of tea and

biscuits, he told Elizabeth about life with the army, the fighting, the casualties, and all the details he wouldn't put on paper but felt relieved to share with his lady. Committing such information to paper risked the intelligence falling into enemy hands. But being able to express his horror at the death and bloodshed, his fear when faced with the need to shoot or be killed himself, and the relief to walk away from a battle without serious injury. That alone was worth the ride to the plantation. Add to that the touch of her lips on his, the clasp of her hand, and the loving smile she aimed his way, and he was in heaven on earth.

"My darling, I must tell you how anxious I am to claim you as my wife. Every day I think about our plans and our future together after the war ends. Which it will before much longer. Everyone says so."

"I do hope you're right on that score." Elizabeth gazed at him, her love evident in the hope and concern in her countenance. "But I am already yours to have and to hold forever."

"And I yours, Elizabeth. Always." He rose to his feet and drew her along with him. He gazed into her silver-flecked blue eyes for several moments. He needed her in a way he had never desired any other woman in his life. He could not imagine ever wanting to be with any woman in the same way he did with the beautiful, caring lady studying him. "I long to show you just how much. We're about to go into battle and I must have the memory of your love to sustain me. Please?"

"What do you mean?" Her question reflected in her eyes as she studied him.

"I realize your father, indeed your family, may not agree with my request. I will not be upset if you deny it. But Elizabeth, my dear, will you lay with me tonight?" He wouldn't have asked if they were not betrothed and promised to one another. If he didn't know to the depths of his soul they belonged together, to support each other, to love each other. He wouldn't have asked if she had ever for one moment acted in any tiny way repulsed by his attentions. The play of emotions flickering across her face reflected her tumultuous thoughts as she considered his brazen request. She peered at him for a long, heart-stopping moment before she slowly nodded.

"I willingly accept your proposal, Jedediah. I've longed for the same thing." She regarded him for several moments and then smiled. "Tonight, come to my bedchamber after everyone is abed."

He kissed her lips, savoring every moment they shared, and pulled back as Jasmine entered the room with a tea tray, followed closely by Lucille. He resumed his place on the couch as Elizabeth sank beside him on the soft cushion. When he looked at Lucille, he saw suspicion in her gaze as she strolled in to take her seat across from the couch.

"I appreciate the hospitality, Mrs. Abernathy." He inclined his head in thanks. "It's quite remarkable how you have managed to maintain a working household despite the scavenging by the troops."

"Indeed. If it weren't for the cleverness of my servants in hiding the best food and drink, along with the cows and chickens in the forest, we'd be destitute like so many others." She contemplated him, gazing at him with a question in her eyes. One she didn't express, but it still unnerved him. "We're fortunate to have faithful hands to know what is important to save. Without any impertinent trouble whatsoever."

Like Elizabeth's reputation? And his appearance? He cleared his throat, as the realization that she suspected why he'd journeyed to see Elizabeth blossomed in his mind. She was a smart, savvy lady; he'd give her that. "I'm sure you are fortunate on that score."

"Aunt Lucille, will you pour?" Elizabeth sat close enough to Jedediah her skirts brushed his breeches. She lifted the plate of pastries to offer to him. "I'm certain Jedediah could use some sweet refreshment to sustain him."

Lucille regarded him for a moment and then

smiled, a knowing grin spreading on her lips. "Of that, I am quite positive."

He accepted a cake and took a bite to keep his lips shut. No secrets would be kept from her. But that didn't mean he'd be forthcoming as to what he and Elizabeth had agreed to share. The less said regarding that matter, the better.

Chapter 8

Charles Town, South Carolina – March 1781

As Elizabeth drove the carriage toward Charles Town, her heart thundered in her chest. She prayed that she and Jasmine could safely pass the sentry without harassment or worse. She kept her focus on the bobbing heads of the pair of horses as they trotted ever closer to the soldier waiting to question her. The soldier who held the power to permit her entry or turn her away.

In truth, she preferred to return to the plantation. She hadn't received any letters from Jedediah in weeks. His parting words of adoration and love after their night together echoed in her mind, invoking the sweeping sensation his final buss had stirred in her core. He'd promised to write when he could and then galloped away to return to the army camp before his deadline. The silence that followed left her worried. Was he hurt? Dead? Would any one inform her if he could not?

"Whoa now." She pulled on the reins to slow the team to a walk, and then to a halt. "Good day, sir."

The loyalist soldier sauntered over to the side of the carriage and held out his hand. "Pass, please."

She reached into her skirt pocket and withdrew the carefully folded page and handed it to him. What if he didn't give it back to her, but tore it up and threw it away? She'd not heard of such an act happening, but there was always a first time. She glanced at Jasmine. Her posture revealed her unease despite her seemingly serene expression. Good thing Emily had stayed back at the manor helping their aunt with reorganizing the linens, in search of holes needing mending. Emily's overactive imagination would have led her to apoplexy. Elizabeth looked back at the soldier in his fine uniform. A stark contrast to the rags the patriots wore. Surely there was something more to be done to help supply them with decent and warm clothing. She must talk to her aunt about the matter when she returned in a few days. But first she longed to see for herself how well her father had fared without the aid of his daughters to run the household.

The soldier regarded her for several moments, looked to Jasmine, and then noticed the burlap sacks and wrapped packages on the rear seat. He raised a brow. "What are you carrying back there?"

Elizabeth swallowed the fear rising in her throat. The meager amount of food and medicine they could scrounge together would only last a few weeks even if they rationed it. But if the soldier confiscated it, they'd have nothing. What would her storytelling cousin Amy do in such a situation? Make up a compelling reason, of course. "Supplies for my father, Captain Joshua Sullivan. He is expecting me to deliver them today for his…important business for the commandant."

"Captain Sullivan?" Doubt crept into the man's eyes. He rubbed a gloved finger beside his nose as he contemplated her statement. His gaze traveled from her to peruse the road behind her. Then he peered at her as he handed back the pass. "Very well. Proceed."

"Thank you." Relief flooded her soul when the man relinquished his objection based on hearing her father's respected name. She pocketed the paper and clucked to the horses, steering them along the road into the main part of town.

The streets were muddy from the recent rain, sucking at the horses' hooves and the wheels of the conveyance. The bombardment and shooting had left their marks on the homes and other buildings throughout the town. Brick homes pockmarked as if they'd suffered some terrible disease. Holes in the streets where heavy cannon balls had fallen. People scurried from place to place, going about whatever business they had but with a chary eye to the enemy troops and officers. Those who remained loyal to the king strolled along as though the town wasn't held by the country's oppressors but their saviors. She shuddered at the sight.

She steered the team through the streets and finally turned into the carriageway leading behind her home to the coach house and stable. A stable hand walked out of the shady interior of the barn to handle the team while Elizabeth and Jasmine clambered out of the vehicle. A pair of hunting dogs nosed about the yard. A couple of chickens pecked the dirt outside the stable. They retrieved the packages from the back seat and hurried across the yard and into the brick building that served as the kitchen situated behind the main house.

"If you'll sort out the food, I'll take the simples into the house." Elizabeth picked through the packages, finally spotting the bundle of medicine packets and the box of bottles of elixirs. Lifting them, she addressed her maid. "Come inside when you're finished here, and we'll see what Father would enjoy for dinner."

"I won't be but a few minutes." Jasmine pulled an apron from a peg on the wall and tied it around her waist. "Some of these will need to be carried to the root cellar for keeping."

Elizabeth shifted the box to a more comfortable grip. "I'll ask Solomon to give you a hand if you need me to?"

"No, miss. I can manage. You go on, and I'll come in when I'm done." Jasmine spun on one foot to deftly sort the bundles and boxes and begin putting the items where they belonged.

Elizabeth made her way outside and across the yard, noting the soft early spring air and the bright blue skies. Wisps of clouds drifted on the slight breeze that carried the scents of the sea and damp soil. As she neared the house, she espied a single candle in each window, unlit. What on earth? They didn't have candles enough for light let alone to put one in every window.

"Father?" She bumped the door closed with one hip and went to the small storage room under the stairs. Placing the box on a shelf and the packets on another one above the box, she strode into the passage to listen for sounds of movement. Hearing a chair scrape on the floor in the front sitting room, she hurried in that direction. "Father?"

"In here." His deep bass floated to her ears as she turned to walk into the room. He rose as she approached him and gave her an embrace in greeting. "I'm glad you arrived safely."

"We had no issues with the sentry. Though he

contemplated taking the small quantities of smoked hams and preserves until he heard your name." Even if it did rattle her comportment for a time, at least she'd managed to get inside the town limits. She had a more pressing question. "Why are there candles in the rear windows?"

"In every window, I'm afraid. Front and back." He raked a hand through his tousled hair, which uncharacteristically was left hanging loose instead of pulled into a queue with a ribbon. "For the illumination this evening."

"What is the occasion for a celebration?" It wasn't a holiday as far as she was aware. She frowned, trying to understand what she was missing.

"The British victory at Guilford Court House on the fifteenth."

"Why would you celebrate such an event?" She frowned at her father as she mulled over his words. Was Jedediah involved in the battle? Was that why she had not heard from him? "You're not actually a loyalist, after all."

"No, but I'm acting as one to keep my home and business safe from British hands." Joshua shook his head, his ebony hair sporting new gray strands brushing his shirt collar. "When the British commander orders an illumination, therefore, I put candles in my windows ready to light when it grows dark. Even if I do not agree."

Her betrothed was out there somewhere fighting for American independence, and her father was celebrating their defeat? Her brothers, too, risked life and limb while she stood in a house that professed to be siding with the British. Maddening. Her father's newly graying hair suggested he felt the same stress of the deception. Oh, to return to the country where she could at least hope for a letter if not a visit from Jedediah. To see him again, safe and whole, remained her most fervent desire. No, mayhap her most fervent wish was to see the end of the war and peace returned to the people and the country.

"How long do you plan to stay?" Joshua strode to the chair he'd vacated upon her arrival and sat, picking up the quill pen in preparation to continue writing. "I miss you and Emily more than I had thought possible. It's quiet without you."

"I'd thought to stay a few days, but now I think I'll return sooner." Back to where she didn't feel the press of British eyes and judgment upon her. "Jedediah has been writing to me at the plantation, and I haven't heard from him in a while. With the news of Guilford Court House, I must fly back to the plantation. I need to be there."

Joshua twirled the feathered pen as he gazed at her, his eyes understanding and kind. "Indeed. What does he say in his letters? Anything of import or just how fond he is of you?"

Heat crept up her neck and into her cheeks. "The latter mostly. He has managed to obtain a pass once to visit for a spell."

Joshua raised a brow and nodded. "I see. I trust you treated him as he deserved for making such an effort?"

"Verily." The image of their lying together played through her mind, increasing the warmth in her cheeks. He had tenderly taught her about the pleasures between a man and woman. Pleasures that could lead to starting a family. The very same pleasures that awakened in her a new sense of what was important to her. Many a bride approached the altar with child from the very same activities she and Jedediah shared. Would she? There was no way to know. "He seemed well pleased by my attentions on his behalf."

"I'm happy to hear that." He regarded her for several seconds and then smiled, dipping the quill into the ink pot. "I agree you should go back to your uncle's to be available should he repeat his effort."

"I'll go to-morrow." She went to her father and hugged his shoulders from behind. She'd go back and wait for her love to come to her side, to show him how much she cared for him. "I'm sure he'll favor me with another such visit when he can arrange it."

Chapter 9

Abernathy Plantation – April 1781

Love and duty warred in his breast as he galloped for the Abernathy plantation in the middle of the month. He'd finally wrangled permission for a lightning fast visit when the army neared the area. But it was only for a night and then he didn't know if he'd ever obtain permission again. General Greene had intimated that the fighting season would be more active than usual. He needed to prepare himself and Elizabeth for that possibility.

The usual ebony-skinned man called out to the house to warn of his approach. A good safety measure to his mind, one that reassured him of the family's defensive practices. Reining to a halt, he leaped from the saddle and tossed the reins to the stable boy as he raced up the front steps. He rapped on the door, then tapped his leg in quick succession. The sound of cattle lowing in the rear of the house reached his ears. A hawk cried in the sky, floating on the spring breeze. After what seemed hours, footsteps approached from inside the house. The door slowly opened, and Jasmine smiled shyly up at him.

"Mr. Thomson, sir, please come in." She opened the door wider and stepped back to allow him inside.

"Greetings. Is Miss Sullivan at home?" He doffed his tricorne and held it between his hands in front of his tattered hunting shirt and stained breeches. His appearance had deteriorated with the prolonged amount of time spent in a tent in camp. But his attire didn't matter as much as his desire to see his love. "I wish to see her, if so."

"Yes, sir. If you'll wait in the parlor, I'll fetch her for you." Jasmine ushered him into the room and then hurried out.

Cooling his heels, he paced. The clock in the tall case at the far end marked each passing second, the ticking seeming to crescendo with each movement of the hands. He counted the knotholes in the floorboards as he walked around the perimeter of the colorful rug. Waiting had never been his strength.

The patter of slippers hurrying along the floor alerted him to someone nearing. He paused his circuit to focus on the open door. Elizabeth fairly skipped into the room, a welcoming smile on her lips and in her eyes.

"Jedediah."

His name on her lips speared desire straight through his heart. He reached out to accept her hands in his, clasping them firmly. "Elizabeth, how fare you?"

"I am well, thank you. What of you?" She inspected him with her gaze. "I was worried when I did not hear from you for so long."

"My apologies, my love. We moved so frequently and were at such a distance that I had no means of sending word." He pulled her close to him, drinking in her pretty features and reveling in her eager acceptance of his touch. But he'd reached a decision in the intervening span. He would respect her enough to deny himself his desire to lay with her again. They'd risked too much the other time. He'd not besmirch her reputation for his carnal needs. "We can hope such will not be the case in the future, but there is no way to guarantee I will be able to send a note or visit again."

"What do you mean?" A slight frown marred her happy countenance. "Where are you going?"

"General Greene has his own idea of how to

fight this war. As much as I wish I could dictate where I spend my time, I have to go where he tells me."

"Until September, is that not right?" She peered at him, slowly blinking as she waited for his response.

"Indeed. Then we can marry." He pressed a kiss to her lips, forcing himself to restrain his passion to something polite and decent.

"Is that a promise?" She tilted her head to one side and squeezed his fingers. "You will leave the fighting then?"

He'd have fulfilled his duty to his country as he had committed to do. He'd fought and bled right along with the other thousands of men defending their cause. He could walk away knowing he'd done what he said he would do to the best of his ability. Then look forward to the rest of his life with the amazing woman gazing up at him with love shining in her eyes.

"That's a promise. But for now, let us enjoy spending some time together before I must away to-morrow."

They spent the rest of the afternoon riding around the fields surrounding the manor, talking about whatever came to mind. Making plans for their future while walking along a merry stream flowing across the corner of one meadow. Hawks screamed as they soared high in the azure sky. A small herd of deer, guarded by a buck, meandered in the distance. He enjoyed the lilt of her voice and the trill of her laugh, foreseeing a pleasant life ahead with her as his companion. They ended up at the manor in time for a late dinner they shared on the back portico overlooking a sweep of lawn as the sun descended.

Lucille Abernathy had assigned him a bed in an upstairs bedchamber at the opposite end of the manor from Elizabeth's room. The woman's expression revealed her continued suspicion of their activities during his previous visit. He had no intention of a repeat performance, so she need not worry. When they all made their way up to their separate chambers around midnight, he pressed a quick kiss good-night to Elizabeth's lips before turning toward his bed.

After he removed his outer clothes, he slipped under the spread and pulled the cover halfway up his torso. It had been a good day, one to remember after he returned to camp. He closed his eyes, listening to the night sounds surrounding the house. How different they sounded from within walls compared to when he slept in a tent, Frank beside him in his bedroll, tossing and turning. After a time, he started to drift off to sleep until he heard a floorboard creak in the hall. Then his eyes flew open and he stared at the door, listening.

The door pull lifted slowly, quietly, and light

seeped between the wood door and jamb as it opened bit by bit. He sat up, braced to defend himself from the intruder if necessary. Only, Elizabeth poked her head around the door and grinned at him, one finger held to her smiling lips. She eased inside, wearing a robe over her shift, and then closed the door as silently as she'd opened it. Turning around, she pressed against it, waiting.

"What are you doing here?"

She sauntered toward him, one slow step at a time. "I want to be with you, Jedediah. Like before."

He shook his head slowly, amazed at her audacity and not wanting to hurt her feelings but needing to keep to his vow to respect her until they did marry. "We shouldn't have lain together last time, my love. I do not believe we should do so again. Your aunt would most definitely object."

She sat on the edge of the bed and gazed at him with expectation in her eyes. "Yes, we should. I want to enjoy our time together as much as possible. Please?" She untied the belt to her robe and slipped the thin material from her shoulders, laying it across the foot of his bed. The moonlight illuminated her face, making her look like an angel.

The little temptress. Oh, how he wanted to as well. But what if she got with child as a result? And then what if he died fighting? How unfair such an event would be for her. He couldn't do it. Not again. He couldn't be that selfish. Not knowing how perilous the next months could prove to be.

She leaned toward him, bringing the scent of vanilla and lavender to his nose. The fall of her long hair across her shoulder called him to run his fingers through the fine tresses. She smiled at him, an enticing gesture suggesting he plant a kiss on her mouth.

"Elizabeth, I do not think it wise." He had to remain strong, to deny his longings and wishes. For her.

"Jedediah…"

The pleading in her eyes was his undoing. He had to find a way to please her without destroying her. "Very well. We can hold each other, but nothing more. I don't want to harm your reputation by creating a child before we are married."

"I'll take what I can get." She moved to slide into the bed with him. "I need to be with you. That is the most important thing."

He wrapped his arms around her; her back pressed to his chest. Felt her breathing gradually slow and his eyes droop. His last thought before sleep claimed him was that he wanted to lie like that forever.

Chapter 10

Abernathy Plantation – June 1781

Sunshine fell upon the blackberry bushes, illuminating the deep purple berries hanging from the fully leafed branches. Elizabeth grasped a plump one and gently tugged it free to place in the basket hanging over her other arm. Emily worked nearby as they slowly moved along the fence row supporting the bushes. Her long muslin skirts dragged across the thorny branches, and she pulled them free with a quick movement.

"I can practically taste the blackberries and cream we'll have for dinner." She quickly slipped berries from their stems and added them to the large basket.

"Too bad Jedediah had to leave weeks before they ripened enough that we could pick them." Emily eased between several long branches to reach the abundance of fruit among them. "Do you fear for his safety like I do for Frank's?"

"Every moment." Elizabeth picked and placed the berries, but her thoughts remained on what her betrothed might be doing at that moment. After their last night together, holding each other until dawn, she had only the occasional short missive to calm her swirling thoughts. "I worry he'll allow his duty to his country to compel him to take risks he need not."

"Both of them are very brave and have vowed to die for the cause if the necessity presents itself." Emily shook her head as she added to her collection. "I do not believe that means they will be foolhardy."

"Men can be boys at times and think they are invincible." The source of her biggest concerns related to Jedediah and Frank, and of course her brothers. At least her sister would not act rashly. Being twins, they enjoyed a deep connection unexplainable by words, only shared feelings. "I'm glad you're here with me, Em. You keep me calm no matter what is transpiring around us."

Emily paused in her berry picking to regard Elizabeth with a serious expression. "My dear sister, you must know that I would do absolutely anything to ensure your happiness and contentment. We are as one in so many respects. You just need to name it and I will always do what I can."

"I know, and I feel the same way. Whatever you need, Em, I'm here to see that it happens for you."

"Now that we have that settled," Emily said, resuming her task, "did you and Jedediah discuss your plan to marry when he was here last?"

"In detail. We must wait until September to have the banns read at church." Such a long time to be forced to wait but she would honor his promise to both the army and to her. "I'll ask that they be read beginning the first Sunday of that month, so the third reading will be completed by the time he is released from his obligation. We'll be joined at the earliest possible date."

"I see you've thought a lot about it." Emily laughed as she moved to work at another bush. "What about your dress? Have you thought about that?"

"I've thought about it, but haven't decided yet on a style let alone the color of the fabric." She sighed, annoyed at her indecision. She wanted the perfect gown, but what constituted the perfect one for her? Then there was the other little consideration. One she had wrestled in her mind for weeks on end before finally coming to a decision of her own. "I'm not sure what size I might need."

Emily turned quizzing eyes to her and halted her hand in midair, abruptly stopping her picking. "What do you mean?"

"One never knows when one may conceive a child." She waited for the shock to register on her sister's countenance. "If it should happen, I mean, then I shall accept my fate with good grace."

"You think you may be with child?" Emily's mouth didn't quite close after she spoke. "You've lain with him?"

"No, and one time. I hope to again, the next time Jedediah visits. If he'll consent as well." She smiled at Emily's surprised features, raised brows, open mouth, suspended hand. "I must convince him of my sincerity in my desire to do so. After all, carrying his child would enable me to have his love with me forever."

"Father will not be pleased with you if you pursue this course of action." Emily recovered from her surprise, her brows drawing into a frown. "I cannot condone your plan."

"As we've discussed, what if he were to die? Then I'd have nothing if not his child to love and nurture. What is amiss with such a desire?"

Emily considered the question for several moments while she plucked berries and laid them on the growing mound in the basket she carried. "I think I understand. While I pray that none of our men die, if Jedediah did then loving his child may be some consolation."

"Indeed. I'd have a part of my betrothed at my side, evidence of my love for him." Elizabeth hesitated as she reached to grip a berry, glancing at Emily. "But I'd rather have them both."

"Naturally." Emily met her gaze. "But one of them is better than none."

Elizabeth nodded, hoping that she would indeed have both. When and if Jedediah came to her again, she'd set the wheels into motion.

Chapter 11

Abernathy Plantation – June 1781

Thank all that was good that his commander understood how desperate he was to be with his woman. It had been too long for his peace of mind since he'd last visited Elizabeth. Jedediah arrived at the plantation knowing he only had the opportunity to return since the army camped nearby for a short time. They might stay in the area for a few weeks, but he would only be able to visit upon occasion, as in when he was not needed. Like this one day. He couldn't even stay the night as he had done before, but that would have to suffice. General Greene proved very generous regarding short leaves as he remembered his own courtship with his wife and how he craved to be in her presence. Otherwise, who knew how long it would have been between visits? Still, if he was one minute late, the general threatened to withhold any more such leaves. Time was of the essence.

As he rode up, he spotted several of the slaves announcing his arrival, acting as protective sentries for the plantation. Several dogs barked to warn him off as well as to announce his presence. He saw Elizabeth and Emily returning from the distant woods with heavy baskets held before them with both hands. It looked like they'd been out picking berries on such a pretty summer afternoon. He saw the moment when they recognized him, suddenly hurrying down the lane, dust kicked up by the hems of their long skirts. He rather liked the simple bonnet tied upon Elizabeth's head, shading her fair features from the sunshine.

They met in front of the manor amidst a flock of disrupted chickens and their complaining squawks. He dismounted, handing the reins to the stable boy, and walked over to greet the ladies.

"Jedediah, I had not expected you." Elizabeth set her basket on the step and crossed the yard to accept his kiss.

"I only have hours, but I had to see you." He shouldn't have kissed her because of the resulting desire shooting through him. But how could he resist those tempting lips? "Miss Emily, how fare you on this fine day?"

"My health is fine, thank you." Emily glanced at him and then Elizabeth, a sly smirk forming on her lips. "I'll take these inside while you talk."

Making good on her words, Emily lifted both baskets, one in each hand. Rather awkwardly, she slowly walked up the steps and through the door, standing open to catch any stray breezes to cool the interior of the house.

"Shall we walk?" He offered his hand and waited for Elizabeth to accept his invitation.

They strolled along the lane, heading toward the stream where a cool breeze brushed his cheek. He enjoyed merely being at her side, not speaking or necessarily even touching. Her proximity brought him peace and tranquility. Calming the ever present urge to be doing something. Being with her was enough.

Three more months of his service and then he'd be free and ready to mesh his life with hers. Three more months of war and the resulting uncertainties. Three more months until his real life could begin.

He squeezed her hand and led her toward a copse of trees, a hidden place where they could be alone and unseen. "The time till we can be together cannot pass quickly enough to suit my taste."

He drew her to him, clasping both her hands to

his chest and kissed her. The surrounding trees stood silent witness to their affection. The temptation proved strong indeed to do more, but he resisted. Holding her fingers linked in his kept his hands from roving her luscious body. She kissed him back, pressing and searching to deepen the connection until he relented. At least for a deeper kiss. Which spurred the desire simmering inside. He couldn't. He broke off the buss and peered into her unfocused eyes. Damnation but she was beautiful and so tempting. So willing. But he'd promised not to disrespect her. Better to wait until they were married.

"Why did you stop?" Elizabeth tilted her head to the side as she gazed at him. She freed her hands from his and placed them on his chest. "You needn't fear that I'd object. I enjoy our busses."

"You know how I feel about waiting." Though his body sure didn't agree with that concept. He gritted his teeth to refrain from acting upon his desires. "We should go back to the house."

She pressed her hands to his chest, holding him from moving away from her. "Jedediah, I want to lie with you again."

A jolt of surprise blended with expectation widened his eyes as he looked at her. "I thought—"

She kissed him, silencing his protest. "If I carry your child as a result, I shall be very happy indeed."

"Your father will not approve in the event." He searched her eyes and found no hesitation or fear of the resulting derision she'd endure. "Why would you risk his wrath?"

The love shining in her eyes as she smiled up at him made his heart fill with emotion. "Because I want to show the world that I love you and this is the best way to declare it. I'll be happy to have your child. So please, lie with me?"

He studied her features, seeing the hope in her eyes, the smile on her lips. She moved her fingers on his shirt, creating little circles of torment on his chest. Pondering his options, he felt his reluctance fade when he considered the number of couples who had welcomed a baby into their family within a short period, mere months, after a marriage. Once a woman accepted a man's proposal of marriage, the contract was binding between them. Given that fact, he saw no reason not to be with his betrothed.

"My love, if that is what will make you content, then I shall do as you ask." Do as he'd longed to do for months. With the woman he couldn't say no to. He bent his head to kiss her, envisioning lying with her upon the soft bed of needles and claiming her as his own.

Chapter 12

Abernathy Plantation – July 1781

The knife in her hand gave her some measure of comfort. Slicing carrots to cook for dinner, Elizabeth fought unwarranted tears. She wasn't slicing onions, after all. Why then the impulse to weep? She couldn't explain it, unless…

Emily strode into the kitchen, a basket of freshly picked strawberries clasped to one hip. She set the basket on the work table and then propped her hands on her hips to peer more closely at Elizabeth. "What's wrong?"

"I cannot fathom why I am crying, but I am." She wiped the dampness from her cheeks with the back of the hand holding the knife.

"Careful there, Elizabeth." Emily reached for the knife, pulling it slowly from Elizabeth's defeated grip. "That's newly sharpened."

Turmoil created a tornado in her chest. She pressed a hand to her stomach and inhaled deeply, releasing the air on a long sigh. The tears. The upset. The lack of her courses. *Wait.* She blinked several times as she stared at her sister, joy and hope blending to calm the whirling winds of emotion inside. Could it be true?

"What now?" Emily tilted her head and lifted one brow, waiting.

A shiver raced down Elizabeth's back, a sign of impending change stirring her senses. "Em, I believe I carry Jedediah's child."

"How can you know?" Emily's querying countenance slowly changed into one of cautious happiness.

"My emotions are all over the place, for one thing." Elizabeth rested both hands on her stomach, certainty replacing the hope she'd felt earlier. "I didn't have my courses as usual either."

Emily smiled and hurried over to clasp Elizabeth's hands with all her strength. "I'm going to be an aunt?"

Elizabeth bobbed her head and squeezed Emily's hands. "I'll be a mother. Oh, Em. I cannot express how filled with joy I am at the prospect. Wait until I tell Jedediah."

When would he manage to get permission to come to her again? She never knew when he'd appear on the carriageway, cantering up to greet her with a kiss and a hug. The uncertainty added to the relief and eagerness she experienced with his surprise appearances. All she could do was continue her round of tasks each day and keep an ear tuned for the sound of hooves on the dirt lane. She bent to her work, but Jedediah was never far from her mind.

Days passed in the summer heat, with nights spent sleeping on the portico to take advantage of the cooler night air. A growing tension pervaded her senses, a feeling of impending doom or disaster. She hated when she had that feeling. It meant something bad was about to happen, but she had no idea what it might be. She could only wait and see.

Emily joined her one morning on the front portico where they'd arranged several comfortable chairs to do their never-ending sewing and mending. The morning sun rose from the back side of the building, so the air remained cooler on the west side until midday. Buzzards slowly circled in the sky, playing on an updraft of warm air with their outstretched black wings. Jasmine carried a tray of cold lemonade out to place on the table between them. The sound of other servants working at various tasks around the manor provided a sense of comfort to her disquieted nerves.

Emily caught Elizabeth's eye as their maid disappeared back into the house. "Do you feel it, too? That something awful is going to occur?"

Elizabeth nodded as she finished tying off the last stitch on the apron she was making. "For a week now, at least. What might it be?"

Emily bit her lip as she shook her head. "I never know, but it's usually something natural, like a storm or fire or whatnot."

Elizabeth relaxed at her revelation. "That's comforting as I feared for our men. That something untoward transpired or is about to happen to them."

"I pray that is not so." Emily resumed her mending of a pair of their uncle's pants. "I cannot imagine them not coming home. But if one of them doesn't, then at least we know he did what he had to for our country."

"Duty and honor in the cause of freedom." Elizabeth frowned at the apron she mauled with her hands. "That is most definitely a cause worthy of a man's life."

"Many have given theirs already." Emily slipped the silver needle through the dark fabric and pulled the thread through to snug the stitch into place. "Uncle Richard believes the end is coming with the victories of General Greene and General Morgan."

"The cessation of hostilities cannot come soon enough." Elizabeth held up the tan apron with its patchwork pockets and carefully folded it to lay it aside. As she turned back to continue their conversation, she heard a pair of horses galloping up the lane toward them.

"We have company." She rose to walk to the edge of the portico to await the men's arrival. The sentry slave hollered out a warning of the impending visitor. The dogs barked as she stood staring down the lane. With each stride of the strong horses, her heart soared higher. "It's Jedediah and Frank. I wonder why they're in such a hurry today."

Emily set aside her sewing and walked over to stand alongside Elizabeth. "It's been too long since we've had the pleasure of Frank's company. I wonder if there is something amiss."

Elizabeth glanced at her sister and then returned her attention to their visitors. "We shall find out soon."

The horses arrived with a cloud of dust as the stable boy ran out to hold the reins as the men swung from their saddles. Crossing the yard with long, hurried strides, they took the front steps two at a time until they stood on the portico in front of Elizabeth and her sister. Dust covered their breeches and smears marred their shirts. Still, they were a most welcome sight.

"Elizabeth." Jedediah pressed a kiss to her lips and then stepped back. "We have but a few minutes before we must fly back to the army."

"What has happened, Jedediah?" She could see the resolve in his expression as well as his love for her. "Why are you and Frank in such a state?"

Frank stood before Emily, his countenance clouded by his concern. "The army is on the move even as we stand here and we must catch up to them before nightfall."

"Where are they headed?" Emily clasped her hands together in front of her skirts, staring up at Frank's serious expression.

Frank reached out to take one of Emily's hands and lift it up to press a kiss to its back. Emily's gaze flew up to meet his, her eyes wide and startled, but she didn't withdraw her hand from his buss. Elizabeth was happy that Frank had finally shown he cared for her sister, a moment that had taken years to arrive. What, indeed, would prompt him to do so at this juncture? It must be something pressing. Dangerous.

"We cannot say for your safety." Jedediah's words drew her attention back to him. "I love you, Elizabeth, and I long for the day when I may claim you as my wife."

She nodded, moved beyond words at the sincerity of his sentiments.

"We came to bid you farewell for a time. We'll be on the move and far from here so unable to return until the fighting is over." Jedediah bussed her lips again, lingering for several beats of her heart before breaking away. "You have my word that I'll do all in my power to return to you, my love."

Heaven above, watch over him. "Jedediah, you must know that I love you and even more important will wait for your return. Come back to me, especially as I believe I carry our child."

Jedediah's eyes flew wide open, and a slow smile crept across his mouth. Just as slowly, his brows descended into a worried frown. "My dear, that is wonderful and awful tidings. Such news provides all the more reason to end this war and return to marry you as we've planned. You must promise to take care of yourself in my absence." He pulled her into a strong embrace, tucking her head to his chest for several moments. When he eased back, he kissed her one last time. "Knowing you will be waiting will goad my efforts to return as quickly as possible."

"We must away." Frank released Emily's hand and smiled at her as he tipped his tricorne. "Be safe, Miss Emily. Miss Elizabeth, you as well. Until such time as we may meet again, fare thee both well."

"Take all necessary precautions until I return." Jedediah tipped his hat with a nod to each of them. Then he spun on one heel and quickly followed Frank.

Once mounted, they paused long enough to wave, and then wheeled their horses and galloped away, a billowing cloud of dust rising behind them, obscuring their departure.

Emily sidled closer to Elizabeth and wrapped an arm around her waist as they lingered there until the dust settled. Until their men had vanished from sight. Then a few moments longer.

"They ride to defend us and the country." Emily sighed and squeezed Elizabeth's waist. "They will be back. They must come back."

Elizabeth blinked away stray tears, refusing to succumb to the pain of Jedediah's departure. She must keep the faith. He would return to her, and their child if she did indeed carry one inside. "I know he loves me and will love our child when he is by my side once again. He must attend to his business, to satisfy his commitment. Then we will enjoy our lives together as we have planned and promised each other. I am content with that knowledge, and can only hope that the time of his return will be very soon."

The End

Thanks so much for reading *Elizabeth's Hope*, the prequel to the A More Perfect Union series! I hope you enjoyed Elizabeth and Jedediah's story. Turn the page for a sneak peek at the next story in the series, *Emily's Vow*!

Sign up. To find out about new releases and upcoming appearances, please sign up for my newsletter by visiting my website or directly at http://eepurl.com/bBE4JX. I only send out a newsletter when I have book news to share with my readers, and that's a promise!

I'd love to hear from you! Feel free to send me an email at betty@bettybolte.com, find me on Facebook at www.facebook.com/AuthorBettyBolte, or connect with me on Twitter @BettyBolte.

You can always find an updated list of the titles in this series, as well as all of my other books, at www.bettybolte.com.

Thanks again for reading!

Sneak Peek of

Emily's Vow

A More Perfect Union

Book One

Betty Bolté

"Frank is due to return any day." Emily Sullivan suppressed a shiver and quickened her pace. If asked, she would blame the early evening breeze blowing inland across the Charles Town harbor for her reaction. Frank had once claimed to be a patriot but now had switched his loyalties to serve as a loyalist broadside printer in the occupied town. How dare he even show his face? Did he truly believe in the British cause or did he have such loose morals as to pretend for his own profit? Either way, she'd have naught to do with the man. Her long skirts swirled about her hurried steps. "I'm glad you wanted to walk with me, Samantha. Your company calms me. And of course it's nicer than traversing the distance home from Aunt Lucille's house with my servants."

"Together we'll be safe enough for such a short walk," Samantha McAlester replied, "though I doubt your father will agree given his insistence that you remain at home."

"It is my fault we left the sewing circle later than I intended, but I miss St. Michael's bells chiming the hour. What shall we do without them? The British should pay dearly for stripping our treasured bells from the steeple."

"Come, let's get you home and off the streets." Samantha quickened her pace.

Emily hurried down the sandy road beside her friend, noting the waning sunshine draping shadows across the street. The slap of the waves at the distant convergence of the Cooper and Ashley Rivers beat a syncopated rhythm against the array of ship hulls, large and small, in the protected harbor. Many of the masts bobbing against the darkening sky sported the hated British flag. The losing army had resorted to sanctioned looting of the beautiful homes—those still standing after two years of British occupation as well as fires and bombardments—as booty for the officers and soldiers before they withdrew. She hoped they would leave soon, but nobody knew exactly when the British ships planned to depart. They'd already sent the bells to London along with other pilfered items. In fact, the British officers sought retaliation for the threat posed by the patriots, who had hidden their true allegiance, against the loyalists living in the city. The officers encouraged harassment of the American citizens, which translated into her father, a leading merchant in town, fearing for her safety more than ever. Until the British actually evacuated, uncertainty and fear blanketed the town.

Dragging in a deep breath, unease settled over Emily's frayed nerves at the thought of Frank's return. "I cannot believe Father insists I marry him after all that man has done. Surely Americans have matured enough they wouldn't force a woman to marry. It's 1782, after all. I'm not a child. Why doesn't he understand?"

A seagull glided past, its laughing call bringing a smile to her face. Her enjoyment didn't last long, though. The occupation of the town created fear and disquiet throughout the citizenry. Add in the horror of her sister Elizabeth's fiancé Jedediah dying, leaving her pregnant and in need of a husband. Then Jedediah's brother Frank, the man Emily had secretly cared for, married her sister to keep the child from being a bastard. Emily survived the misery of watching Frank marry Elizabeth only to suffer much more when Elizabeth died in childbirth with Frank away at war. Emily had come to terms with the prospect of raising her nephew, but being forced into marriage with Frank, too? How could life turn and twist with such disregard for her future goals and plans?

Frank's imminent arrival now distressed her as much as the three hundred British ships crowding the harbor. The rumor about town suggested the ships stood poised to carry away the defeated enemy troops along with any loyalists wanting to flee the town. Many slaves would likely take the chance on freedom offered by the British, despite the American protests. The constant motion of the water for once failed to soothe her troubled thoughts.

"Have you told your father how you feel?" Samantha matched Emily's stride easily despite her slight limp and the basket she carried.

Sharing her feelings with her father had once enjoyed an easy place in Emily's heart. Now his demands for her to cloister within the theoretic safety of the town house, joined with his desire that she marry to secure her future, made confiding in him difficult. His concern stemmed from her advancing age with few appropriate prospects for marriage due to America's fight for its independence from an overbearing mother country, which seemed to be winding down. She longed for those carefree days, years before, filled with friendly banter and heartfelt discussions with her father.

Emily wrinkled her nose. "I haven't spoken with him, not that I think he'll care. He's more concerned with my supposed need for a protector while he's away." What a pickle. Did he have to choose Frank to serve as both bodyguard and suitor?

The thought created ripples of fear along her spine. Marrying a man, any man, meant losing her individuality, a fate she dreaded. The vows included obeying and honoring him, which translated into having his children. She shivered, recalling her twin sister on her deathbed mere days after delivering her son. Emily held her hand as

Elizabeth's life departed, her fingers falling limp within Emily's clutching grasp. Just like their mother before her.

So many young women across the country feared pregnancy and being brought to bed for that very reason. Elizabeth, like many of those women, had written out her will when she discovered she carried a child. At least the document detailed her wishes for her son. And her surrogate husband, Frank Thomson. Elizabeth was to wed Jedediah, the betrothal announced and celebrated, before Elizabeth revealed she was with child. The banns had been read twice when his militia duty arose and he'd left to fight. If Jedediah hadn't been killed, Frank would not have felt obligated to do his duty as Jedediah's brother to wed Elizabeth and give the unborn child a father and thus avoid bastardy.

Emily used to think of him as *her* Frank, until he told her his decision to wed Elizabeth. Her heart had hurt for months as she struggled to understand and accept the reality that she could never have him. But once Elizabeth died in similar circumstances as their mother, Emily's fear of dying as a result of childbirth eclipsed any naive desire to marry.

No, better to pursue her dreams of opening her ladies' accessories shop. She squared her shoulders, ready to face the astonishment of the ladies in town as well as plan a strategy for the battle when her father voiced his objections.

Lost in thought, Emily slowed involuntarily as Samantha paused in front of the empty bakery, its door shut tight. Next door the printing office boasted the glow of lanterns through the windows, signaling someone working late to prepare the British broadside for the morrow. Emily turned her attention back to the vacant bakery. She loved the little building so full of wonderful memories. Signs posted in the two plate-glass windows flanking the front door vainly tempted passersby with blueberry or cranberry muffins, apple pie, or pumpkin bread. She inhaled expectantly. Tears smarted her eyes when she smelled only sea salt and wood fires.

"I cannot believe they actually hung the poor Widow Murray," Samantha said. A gust of wind snagged a few strands of ink-black hair, tugging them free from the casually wound bun nestled inside her bonnet. She tucked the strays behind one ear and glanced at Emily.

"It is not surprising, when you consider her penchant for gossip, now is it?" Emily stopped also. The stooped woman had delighted in sharing titillating chitchat while Emily selected her two loaves of bread. Mischievous, she was, cackling over another's indiscretion. The woman refused to be circumspect, saying more than acceptable once too many times. But to be hung by the British as a spy? The foul Britons had no respect for American ladies.

The darkened shop sat cold and lonely compared to the once-bustling business. A chill skated down Emily's spine, and she hugged herself. The Widow Murray had survived the death of her husband at the fight for Stono Ferry in June of 1779, and her bakery served as a popular early morning and late afternoon stop for the townspeople, until the British invaded Charles Town in May 1780. Then everything changed.

Sadness mixed with anger settled in the pit of her stomach. She missed her brothers, off fighting with the militia, but at least their efforts yielded the nearing peace. "And to think, she stopped three deadly attacks on our boys just by sharing with my father what she heard."

Samantha shrugged. "Yes, but it still makes me sad."

"Her little shop feels so abandoned." Emily squinted at the store, assessing its size and features. The quaint store sat along a normally busy thoroughfare that promised to provide plenty of potential customers after peace returned. But first, she had to find the right moment to share her intentions, starting with her cousin Amy Abernathy and Samantha. Amy was her strongest ally and thus the perfect person to stand with her. Second, find a way to tell her father. After all, her new resolve to take care of herself unfortunately still required his assistance to secure the shop, given contracts were men's domain. Convincing her father she meant to conduct business on her own presented a nearly insurmountable challenge, but she would find a way to do so. Then she'd have to share her plans with the ladies in the sewing circle in order to garner their support of her efforts. She already envisioned mannequins within the cool dimness behind the glass panes, displaying embroidered dresses, shoes, slippers, and gloves. She pictured herself waiting on customers, sweeping up scraps of floss and fabric from her sewing, keeping the windows shiny clean.

Peering at the empty building, she sighed. The stone and wood-plank structure invited passersby through its half-glass door. Large glass windows would allow the sunlight to filter inside, illuminating the interior in a way that made Emily smile with pleasure. She wanted to set up shop immediately. Her father would resist allowing her to do such a daring thing, citing society's expectations of women. Marriage, children, housework. No mention of a proper education nor avenues to personal achievement in the merchant world. Her father's stature in the community dictated her options, limited such as they were. She wanted more than a clean house and a productive garden from life. Somehow, she must persuade him to see reason.

With a long last look, Emily turned away from the temptation of the store. "We must go. I don't want my father to catch me here without his required escort, and we're very late as it is."

Few other people ventured onto the street as darkness crept closer and the stars began to wink at her from above. A lone wagon lumbered by, pulled by a dapple-gray draft horse, its ribs clearly visible in the evening light. Emily's heart went out to the beast. Even the horses suffered from want of adequate food, much like the townspeople. The prices of food and wares had increased a thousand percent since the onset of the war. The Continental Congress embargoed staples such as rice, indigo, corn, beef, and pork to ensure the American armies had provisions. If it weren't for her father ignoring those embargoes and continuing to export rice and indigo to the West Indies and France, they too would suffer financial distress. He also imported goods for sale in town, enabling them to continue to purchase food despite the exorbitant cost.

In years past Charles Town had bustled at this time of day. The town's women would have been chatting together while strolling to the marketplace, once replete with a variety of foods and wares. The men engaged in heated discussions on their way to McCrady's tavern for a pint after a day spent at the Exchange conducting business. Wagons and carriages rumbled along to the steady rhythm of horses' hooves, creating puffs of dust to drift up and settle on the long skirts and pants of those on the street. All under the watchful eyes of the seagulls soaring and screaming overhead.

Danger patrolled the streets in the form of British soldiers searching for anyone who dared be a patriot within the town limits. Those who had not signed the loyalty oath to King George's dictatorial ways were either run out of town, their property confiscated, or imprisoned on the ships at anchor in the harbor. Indeed, one night in August 1780, several prominent patriots, including Governor John Rutledge's brother, Edward, and Peter Timothy, the editor of the *Gazette*, found themselves charged with seditious activities, arrested, and sent to the St. Augustine prison in British East Florida. They were released after a year or so, but instead of being allowed to return to their homes in Charles Town, they were sent to Philadelphia to be with their exiled families.

Samantha gripped the basket's arched handle with both hands and shrugged. "Your father will chastise us no matter, so what's the point?"

"At least I can honor his request by being home before night completely falls. He objects to me being on the street, but my skills are needed. The cloth and shirts we're sewing will make our soldiers' lives a little more bearable. Perhaps even one of my brothers will receive comfort, wherever they are now." A seagull swooped onto the street in front of Emily, and she shooed it away with her skirts. Looking down the shadowy lane, she tensed. "Fiddlesticks, I'd hoped to avoid this."

Two British soldiers, replete in crimson coats boasting dark blue facings and white breeches, ambled up the street, their rifles slung over their shoulders, bayonets sheathed. The two men saluted a third—a loyalist officer, by the hated dark blue coat faced with white and the crossed white straps—as they neared him on the opposite side of the road. To her mind, loyalists were worse than the British regulars because they chose a distant, controlling king over their friends and, in many cases, their own families.

"Quick, while they are busy," Samantha whispered as she pulled her bonnet closer around her face, though she kept an eye on the men. "Perhaps they won't notice."

Emily's heart sank. She'd gone and done it now. Her father would skin her like a rabbit if she landed in trouble. Again. Try as much as she did, she seemed to invite mischief. She furtively watched the men engage in a brief exchange. Solidly built, they stood as tall as young saplings, their broadcloth uniforms stretched taut over massive chests. One soldier winked at her with a slow, hungry leer as they approached. She lowered her head so the bonnet shaded her face but still allowed her to watch their actions. "I fear it's too late. Surely, though, they won't harm us standing on a public street."

She glanced at the men, the lanterns they carried casting wavering light across their faces, alarm sparking inside her at the hungry amusement on their faces. She grabbed Samantha's arm and started down the sandy road. Her heart beat a staccato rhythm when the men neared, intercepting the two women on the nearly deserted street. As the soldiers drew to a halt in front of them, a low, menacing chuckle from the taller of the men sent terror snaking down her back.

"Now, now, ladies, don't be in such a hurry," the first soldier said, blocking her path.

He reached out to tug loose a string from her tea-colored bonnet, her last decent one. She'd pulled it from her mother's trunk, forced to use even those last remaining articles of clothing. The filth. Bad enough they were British. Emily recoiled, gagging at the odor of sweat and tobacco. She swatted his hand away. The major—from the insignia she could now see far too closely— approached them. Something in his eyes, glittering beneath his hat, tugged at her memory. She dared not investigate more for fear he'd misinterpret her look as one of interest. She glanced away but kept an ear on the soldiers' movements.

"They just want to have some fun," he said, his voice sharp as he stepped closer. "Where is your father, Miss Sullivan? Surely he didn't allow you to venture out alone?"

"He's awaiting my return, if you'll permit me to pass." Emily made to continue on her way, but the officer raised a hand, stilling her movement.

"Not yet. We merely wish to speak with you, make your acquaintance. After all, there's no one to stop us, now is there?"

"I will." Samantha planted her feet and gripped the basket with both hands, glaring at the men.

She would, too. Samantha proved the strongest of her friends, capable and confident. Emily often wished for Samantha's fortitude. Where had she learned to confront an adversary with such confidence?

The officer chuckled. "It would be fun for you to try, at least. Perhaps then your father will mind his business ventures with more care."

Samantha's eyes narrowed at his comment, but she held her ground. "We are late, sirs. Please, let us pass."

"We'll not detain you for long. I only want to taste a young lady one more time before I board one of those ships for England," the first soldier said, leaning closer to Emily and laying a hand on her arm to restrain her. "You're such a pretty little blonde, too." He snatched the lace-trimmed bonnet from her head.

She gritted her teeth when he mauled her mother's delicate bonnet. "That's mine!" Emily grasped at it, clutching air until finally finding purchase on the hat, and pulled it from his smudged fingers. With shaking hands, she straightened the lace-edged brim as the man chortled at her predicament. She inhaled to calm her roiling stomach. "Gentlemen, please."

Seething, she inspected her hat. At a minimum, he fouled it by his touch. Bad enough the town ran thick with thousands of enemy soldiers without having to deal with these animals. Her hands trembled, but she steeled herself to face the loathsome men. She relied upon what little decency they may possess to help Emily and her friend out of this precarious situation. "Young ladies, as you say, prize their virtue and thus do not share kisses with strangers. If you'll step aside, we'll continue on our way home."

The second soldier yanked the bonnet from her hands and lifted it to his nose, inhaling deeply. "Love the smell of a fine woman."

The man rubbed her bonnet on his face, inhaling deeply each time it swiped across his nose. A dark smudge appeared where he'd wiped his grimy face on the lightweight fabric. She swallowed the bile rising in her throat. Suddenly footsteps echoed behind her, but she dared not tear her eyes from her assailants to turn to see who approached. Might it be yet another foul British soldier attacking from the rear? The apprehension pounding in her ears along with her pulse prodded her into action. She refused to believe anyone would take advantage of her, not in her own town on the eve of independence.

If Samantha could defend herself, then so could Emily. Gripping the strings of her purse tightly, she swung it in a large arc at the closest soldier, hitting him on the elbow with a loud crack. Good, the tin of snuff she'd purchased for her father had earned its worth this day.

"Gramercy, woman, watch what you do there." The soldier rubbed the injured joint, scowling. "I just wanted a little kiss or two. No need to get angry."

"Let us pass unharmed like gentlemen should or I'll hit you again." Breathing hard, she pulled back to deliver another blow when a hand gripped her upper arm and stayed her movement. The heat from the gloved hand seared her where it lay.

"I'll thank you to leave the ladies alone, *gentlemen*. And I use that word loosely." The deep, familiar voice sounded above her head, sparking nearly dead embers of feeling in her core.

She knew that voice. She heard it in her dreams

on too many nights and had dreaded hearing it again in person. Its timbre reverberated against her chest, a physical caress as he stepped behind her close enough his heat warmed her back. Relief mixed with despair as a jolt of recognition flowed into her body, tempting her to lean against his powerful frame.

Emily glanced over her shoulder at the tall blond. Light from the open printing shop door pooled onto the ground behind him. Her pulse quickened at the sight of him standing behind her. Her lips parted, remembering his touch, a fleeting touch that had started a feeling like a bubbling creek in her veins, a longing in her heart and inner core she did not fully comprehend.

Frank.

Here.

She snapped her mouth closed, afraid she might reveal too much of the intense physical response she experienced when he touched her. She braced herself against the onslaught of emotions he stirred within her, attempting a frown to show her displeasure. But…

His dove-gray eyes enthralled her. She could lose herself in their tantalizing depths. When he winked at her, her breath hitched. She broke eye contact and turned to face forward.

"I believe you have something of the lady's." Frank held out a hand to the soldier, snapping his fingers as he silently demanded the garment. His steady gaze made the soldier shove the bonnet toward Frank before hastily stepping back several yards, well out of range of any physical response. Emily grimaced. Did everyone jump when he snapped his fingers? He may be surprised when she did not.

Frank handed the bonnet to her with a grim expression and a nod. Although still heavenly to look at, with lush, sandy-blond hair, chiseled jaw, and steely gray eyes, now a hardness surrounded those eyes, his firm mouth. He seemed taller, broader, more capable than nine months earlier, before he left town after his swift marriage to Elizabeth.

She folded the offending garment and glared at the circle of men dwarfing her. Why must he show up now? After all this time away from home. Her heart skipped a beat, then restarted wildly with a crazy mix of joy and resentment. Where had he been when her home life fell apart?

Still, at least for right now, he was here, protecting her from these buffoons. And her father's subsequent anger, should aught go awry. She'd sacrifice her pride *this* time. She sidled behind him, placing his bulk between her and the aggressors.

The major assessed Frank's height and size, his look changing from antagonistic to resigned when he noted the insignia on his uniform.

"What right do you have to interfere?" the first soldier asked Frank, seeing the change in the major's demeanor. "We were here first."

"Lieutenant Colonel Nisbet Balfour himself requested my presence. And this lady's father is my father-in-law, who charged me with ensuring the ladies' safe passage."

Frank knew the hated colonel? The very man who had personally succeeded, through his intolerant and hateful attitude, in alienating many of the surreptitious patriots in Charles Town. They were forced to sign a fealty oath to King George or be run out of town. On top of that, Frank admitted he had already talked with her father. She had wanted more time before Frank returned. Time to face her father's unrealistic dreams for her. Time to take the steps necessary to open her own shop and determine how she would proceed with her plans. If she were to be truly independent, then she must insist on being treated as such. Frank's officious behavior stroked her irritation.

"We'll see about that," the soldier said, surging forward and aiming his rifle at Frank.

Emily gasped, gripping Frank's cloak involuntarily. He set her from him then stepped forward, drawing the man's attention and the path of his aim away from her. Frank braced his feet as he faced the frustrated soldier. "Be sensible, man."

Trembles rocked her to the core at the tableau

playing out before her. Motion slowed to a crawl as she attempted to make sense of the scene. Her breath caught in her throat as the seriousness of the situation sank into her rattled brain.

The man stalked toward Frank, his finger on the trigger of the weapon. Huge paws hung at the end of the soldier's muscular arms. Thick fingers curled around the dark wood stock and supported the long metal barrel. Stubble shadowed his jaw and surrounded his yellow smile. The rifle aimed at Frank's abdomen. "I'll have what I came for and you cannot stop me."

At this close range, even if he tried, he couldn't miss. She fixed her eyes on Frank, saw when his eyes turned to mirrors, focused on settling the challenge. He appeared capable of killing her assailant then and there. Cold fear lodged in her chest. Frank came home, only to be shot? Over a bonnet? No. She wouldn't allow it. She made to take a step to intervene, stop the madness, but Samantha grabbed her arm with a fierce grip all while shaking her head. Emily tried to ignore her, but her friend held fast.

"I believe the lady has a say in the matter." Frank whipped a pistol from some hidden place, cocked the hammer with a deadly *click*, and leveled it at the man. "I'd think again about your intentions, sir."

Emily tugged on Samantha's hold. "Frank, no!"

Frank locked eyes with his opponent, his thumb ready to release the lethal ball. His eyes narrowed, intent and deadly.

"Stand down, soldier," the major cut in. "This has gone far enough. Next thing you'll be challenging him to a bloody duel over nothing more than a thwarted buss."

"Put your gun away," Frank said to the soldier, "or face charges of assaulting an officer."

The soldier reluctantly cradled his gun, glaring at Frank.

"Are you Captain Thomson, by chance?" the major asked, scrutinizing him.

"Yes, sir," Frank said slowly. He lowered his pistol, keeping it handy.

"Colonel Balfour mentioned you were to arrive to take over the printing press and the broadside." The major considered Frank and the lethal weapon, his internal debate evident in his expression. "But your point is well-taken. This is neither the place nor the time." He turned to address the soldiers. "All right, men, return to your duties."

"But sir—" The man's voice held a barely concealed whine.

"You heard him. Move along now." Frank replaced his pistol, though he did not relax his demeanor. Might they be safe and allowed to continue, or would there be some retaliation? Emily would fight, at least verbally, for Frank if she must. Her actions had incited this predicament, so she felt compelled to help resolve it. Fortunately, the officer quelled the whiner's eagerness with a severe look before tipping his hat to Emily and Samantha.

"Ladies, my apologies," the officer said slowly. "You may be on your way."

"Thank you for your assistance." Frank studied the officer as the disgruntled soldiers stalked away. Still he stood ready to defend himself if called upon to do so.

"One moment, sir." Samantha's eyes flashed as she gripped the basket handles. Fury simmered beneath her words. "What? No reprimand for your men?"

"Ladies." The officer smirked at her questions, then followed the two soldiers down the street.

Taking a deep breath, Emily faced Frank.

Frank's dark gray eyes turned stormy, his hands on his hips as he studied her.

"Pray tell what you two are doing on the street alone?"

The next morning, Emily endured Frank escorting her to the sewing circle, acquiescing to her father's outraged insistence. He argued with her about the necessity of her attending, and she'd finally convinced him to permit her to go, but only if Frank walked with her to prevent any further attempts on her virtue and welfare. They stopped to pick up Samantha from her home on the way which made the walk bearable.

Emily paused at the edge of the street and scanned the facade of Aunt Lucille's three-story brick house, shading her eyes from the sun. The lovely home stood in the middle of the block, with its courtyard of flowers and bushes below the upper piazzas. Two of her father's Negroes, Richard and Solomon, had lugged the necessary equipment and supplies from home to her aunt's house on Meeting Street, a double dwelling similar to the Sullivan home overlooking the wharfs and harbor on Bay Street. Fortunately the men were among the few who did not take the chance when tempted with freedom as long as they fought for the British. Although liberation from slavery lured many blacks into the battle, rumors abounded that the slaves who did so ended up slaves elsewhere afterward. Thus many blacks stayed with the families they knew rather than trade for a worse situation. Richard and Solomon were like kind uncles to Emily, both having lived with the Sullivans her entire life.

Emily and Samantha, along with a brooding Frank, entered through the street door to the first-floor porch. The young men's strength had apparently made quick work of the assembly of the loom. Emily greeted her personal slave, Jasmine. She had tasked the young black woman with carrying the spindles of flax thread used to weave the cloth and also in directing Richard and Solomon in their chore. Now the loom stood ready for Emily to take her seat and start the shuttle flying back and forth to weave the linen fabric. The men's immediate labor completed, they retired to the cooking kitchen to "assist" the women with preparing the midafternoon lunch for the ladies, while Jasmine helped with the sewing. The sound of the black women singing as they worked in the kitchen behind the house complemented the whir and chatter in the parlor.

Emily settled on the small seat of the loom, and placed her feet on the treadles, pressing them in a steady rhythm. She sent the shuttle's smooth wood sliding easily between the vertical threads, weaving the flax into cloth. With each toss of the shuttle, left, then right, then left, Emily thought of her three brothers and the other men still fighting. Small skirmishes continued to erupt whenever the militia happened upon scavenging British troops confiscating whatever provisions they deemed necessary from the surrounding plantations and homes.

"I imagine Frank's temper showed after you and

Samantha behaved so boldly yesterday." Amy paused in her passage across the room to stand beside Emily. Cousin Amy's dark copper tresses cascaded down her back, catching the firelight, while her emerald eyes sparkled with mirth above porcelain cheeks.

Whirring spinning wheels hummed a tune as background to the conversations in the large upstairs parlor of Aunt Lucille's home. The requisite fire kept the cool October air at bay. Emily passed the shuttle to and fro, glancing over to where Samantha now sat by the cozy fire stitching a sleeve onto a shirt. The room overflowed with women, white and black, free and slaves, working together to provide warm, sturdy clothing to the men fighting to defend their independence from King George III.

Emily paused in the act of throwing the flying shuttle and pumping the treadles to pat her kerchief across her damp brow. She grinned at the memory of Frank's dark scowl as he hustled them down the street the night before. "A tad, but he soon recovered, I daresay. His displeasure spoiled his handsome face when he realized Samantha and I had walked together through town." More like outraged, but he had contained his ire with her. "He's gone to McCrady's Tavern to meet Father on some business or other."

"I'm pleased, Cousin, that you arrived safe."

Amy hugged her briefly before stepping back to gauge her condition. "The British and loyalists are desperate enough to seek vengeance on anyone who crosses them."

Emily could only nod in silent acknowledgment. The chasm of fear that had opened within her when the soldiers accosted them would forever remain her secret. And when Frank had faced certain death, her heart nearly stopped beating. Those few minutes of uncertainty she and Samantha agreed to keep to themselves, given no good could arise from telling anyone about the men's inappropriate actions. It was bad enough her father had to be told. Frank's lecture all the way home had done nothing but vex her and spoil the evening.

Amy's mother, Lucille Abernathy, glided to join them, making a path through the organized chaos inherent with the sewing apparatuses and materials strewn about the large room. Her mud-brown day gown sported a flowered apron with two pockets filled with thread, needles and lace. Her gray-streaked black hair swept up to a bun with a white cap perched on top. The years of war had imprinted worry lines, radiating from the corners of her mouth in contrast to the sparkle of her eyes.

"It is dangerous for two young women to be alone in town, especially now," Aunt Lucille said.

"You should have walked with Richard and Solomon from here to your house."

"I'm sure Father would agree with you." Emily surveyed the room, taking a few moments to stifle the annoyance bubbling within her. It all sounded so easy to rely upon some man being with her in order for her to do anything. But it rankled deep inside her soul to be forced to wait for a proper escort even though that was expected. Annoyance simmered within her at the prolonged war with the British, at being treated like a child when she was nearing twenty-five and headed for spinsterhood, and most of all for not knowing exactly when Frank would return so she could have avoided running into him at all. To learn he served as the new printer for the remaining months of the British occupation, and thus working next door to where she planned to rent a shop, made matters even more upsetting. "Next time, mayhap I will let them escort me."

"Next time Frank shall escort you, now that he's back in town. After all, Frank is a nice man, honest and fair." Aunt Lucille slipped her hands into her apron pockets. "And able to look after those he cares about."

"I suppose." She refused to think of Frank as more than her sister's husband—or widower now. He had chosen Elizabeth when a choice needed to be made. All for little Tommy's sake. Then why did her heart race so at the thought of Frank being nearby again? She mentally shrugged away the question. Likely she experienced indigestion at his unwanted presence. Whether attracted to him—an absurdity—or not, she no longer desired to encourage relations with a man. Her own plans did not include marriage, no matter how handsome or smart the man might be. Not any longer.

Jasmine crossed the room and waited for Emily to acknowledge her. "Your tea is waiting downstairs as requested, miss."

After thanking Jasmine, Emily beamed at Amy. Time to reveal her plans to her confidantes. "Aunt Lucille kindly allowed me to arrange a private tea for us. I have a surprise I'd like to share with you and Samantha."

"Now?" Amy scanned the busy room, then pinned her gaze on Emily. "We have much to finish."

"I cannot wait any longer." Her determination wavered as she contemplated the enormous task before her, not only in terms of starting a business. The bigger challenge rested in gaining the acceptance by her community when she pushed the boundaries of propriety in such a bold manner. The next step after securing her father's assistance, of course, would be discussing her plans with her circle of friends, the ladies in this room. They had stood by her throughout Elizabeth's confinement,

childbirth, illness, and then funeral. The patriotic
women would also have the ability to smooth over
the idea with their husbands and fathers. Before
she did that, she needed to know her cousin and
friend supported this most difficult decision.

"You've always liked a good mystery." Amy's
eyes lit with curiosity as she followed Emily across
the room. Upon Emily's invitation, Samantha
quickly agreed to the clandestine tea party.

They adjourned to the downstairs library at the
front of her aunt's house. The tall, shuttered
windows protected the inhabitants both against the
dust rising from the sandy street beyond and from
prying British eyes. A wood fire crackled and
hissed in the fireplace.

Emily poured chamomile tea into flowered cups
and set the china pot down before gazing at Amy
and Samantha, who waited for her to speak. What
to say? She'd longed for the courage to broach this
topic for a week, hesitating to reveal her innermost
desires even to her closest confidantes for fear of
their reaction. Lifting the porcelain cup to her
mouth, she sipped, debating how best to share her
news. On a sigh, she set the cup and saucer down.

"I've decided to open an embroidery shop." The
words tumbled from her mouth. Amy and
Samantha stared, mouths dropping open at the
announcement. Emily suppressed the nervous
laugh that threatened. She twisted the tiny gold

mourning ring on her right hand, silently asking Elizabeth for her understanding. She took a deep breath and let it out in a rush. "I do not want to be a wife and mother. Rather, I'll support myself and live the way I wish."

Gasps expressed their surprise. Closing her mouth, Amy eased her cup onto the saucer and gazed at Emily before laughing. "You cannot be serious, Em. A spinster? You? You've always wanted a large family and a loving husband. You mustn't tease us this way."

"I'm not joking. I do not wish to be owned by a man." Emily clenched her hands until they turned white at the knuckles. Not even by Frank, the man she once loved with all her heart. A quiver of remorse fluttered within her chest as she blinked back gathering tears.

"Owned?" Samantha gazed steadily at her. "Come now, you do not believe such folly, surely. A husband is not a slave driver."

"Pshaw. I've seen how men treat their wives." Emily dabbed her kerchief at the corner of her eyes. "How fathers give away their daughters with their dowry and little more than a kiss good-bye and good riddance. I'll not do it, I tell you."

"I cannot believe what I'm hearing." Amy shook her head, rising from her seat and pacing past the carved mahogany bookcase filling one long wall. She stopped by a round table with its cut-glass decanters of maroon port and amber sherry and four glasses. Toying with the lace doily, she said, "You cannot believe your father would allow you to forgo marriage and children. You know he won't support you forever."

"He won't have to," Emily said. "For once, Father must understand my position."

"But Em, this is simply not done. You know this is impossible."

"It should not be impossible. Can't you see? I cannot risk having children." Emily felt her heart contract in disappointment. She fiddled with the gold band, recalling her childhood dreams of robust sons and lovely, precocious daughters to help her and love her in her dotage. But no more.

"All because of Elizabeth's death?" Samantha asked softly. She moved to stand near Emily and peered into her eyes. "Is that what you're afraid of?"

Emily searched Samantha's eyes, willing her to understand. "First my mother and now my sister perished after birthing children." A tremor coursed through her. Her dear twin, Elizabeth. How she missed her happy chatter and caring ways. "Samantha, you as a midwife know even better than I do how many women die in childbirth. I dare not risk it."

Amy paced the lavishly furnished room. Her homespun skirts brushed her ankles as she turned at each corner of the oriental carpet, avoiding the cushioned sofas and side chairs. "But, my dear, it's simply not permissible for ladies of our station to be shopkeepers. If I know Uncle Joshua, he will be furious once he hears of this ridiculous notion of yours."

"Why is it ridiculous?" Emily drew herself up to her full height. "Other women have shops in town. The Widow Murray's bakery was one. Mrs. Dunwoody has that lovely fashion store over on Market. And, and…"

She racked her brain for other examples, but few women desired to be independent. The coverture laws provided for wives to be supported throughout their lives. Unmarried women were merely a burden on the family, and thus encouraged or even required to marry to remove the burden and be a useful member of society. Indeed, most women wanted to be homemakers and care for their families. They only worked in shops when forced to take over their husband's business upon his death or face starvation. Raised themselves with the expectation of marriage, children, and household chores, many looked on spinsters as neglecting their duty to marry and perpetuate mankind. With a wry smile, Emily realized she used to be one of them. No more. With the death of Elizabeth, her opinion had changed.

She snapped her fingers as more female merchants came to mind. "Mrs. Johnson sells candles and scented sachets over on Broad," Emily said. "Surely I can open a shop and sell decorated hats and gloves. My embroidery and weaving skills are both respected in town, so I shall make clothes and embellish handkerchiefs, satin shoes, even wedding dresses. I don't believe there is anything wrong with having a shop, after all. Women should have as much right as men to earn a living."

"I don't entirely disagree with you, Emily. However, while women can help in the shops, only widows can inherit the shop from their husbands, not maidens. We cannot even own property until we're widows." Samantha laid a hand on Emily's rigid arm. "Relax, my dear. We're not criticizing."

"No? It feels that way." Withdrawing from Samantha's touch, she strode to the fireplace. Thoughts cascaded through her mind, tumbling freely with rampant emotions into an intricate knot that settled in the pit of her stomach. Amy and Samantha wanted the best for her and spoke the truth about the difficult path ahead. The challenges and sacrifices she faced made her more determined to succeed.

Amy crossed the room and sank gracefully onto the settee facing the fireplace. She arranged her skirts around her. The thump of Amy's hand on the needlepoint cushion invited Emily to join her. "Em, please, come sit and let us discuss this rationally."

Emily did not move. A *pop* and *hiss* from the fire echoed through the silence. She could not move. She needed them to understand, not oppose her choice. If they couldn't accept and support her decision, she despaired of ever convincing the ladies sewing circle and even less her father. Her heart beat in her ears as she took two slow breaths.

Amy patted the brocade cushion once more. "Em, please. Sit here with me."

Something rigid in her spine relented. With a sigh, Emily went to sit beside her. She settled her skirts, though never as beautifully and effortlessly as Amy, who long ago perfected the art of entertaining and welcoming others no matter where she went. Emily could not hope to achieve the ease with which Amy spent her life. Being sociable came naturally to Amy. She attracted suitors as easily as a net collected fish, and Emily worried her cousin's particular style of fishing would simply lead to more troubles.

"Talk to me." Amy laid a hand on top of Emily's clenched ones. "What is truly happening?"

Emily stared into the fire for a moment before addressing Amy's question. Her hands trembled in her lap, and she pressed them together. "If I marry,

I will be expected to have children, lots of them, no less, to support our young country. I understand what's expected but I would jeopardize my very life. It's not what I wish for my future."

"And?" Amy asked gently. "There's more to this story, I believe."

Her heart sank. Emily regretted confiding in her cousin her feelings for and initial intensely physical reaction to Frank. His touch on her fingers, coupled with the light kiss on the back of one lucky hand, had created a sizzling sensation throughout her body, leaving her hungry and longing when he'd stepped away. Then the ensuing devastation when he proposed marriage to Elizabeth. Recovering from the fracture in her heart proved a long, painful process, but she had managed. That episode would stay in the past, where it belonged. She squared her shoulders and searched Amy's eyes silently, trying to convey her feelings without having to put voice to them. "I don't know what you mean."

Amy's hand tightened on hers, and her lips curved slightly. Emily closed her eyes and sighed, a tear crawling down her cheek. She brushed it away.

No tears. No more.

"I understand," Amy said slowly. "I, too, do not wish to marry. I'm not afraid of having children, mind. But to give up what I want to do to be subservient to a man who has all the rights and privileges of this new country while I sit by and have nothing to my name?" Winding the long auburn curl hanging beside her jaw around her index finger, Amy stared thoughtfully into the fire. "I see your point, Cousin. Perhaps it is best to be a spinster by choice and suffer the townspeople's insults than to be forced to remain at home, subject to the vagaries of men."

"What did you say?" Emily peered at Amy. Her cousin, who loved to flirt and dance, would willingly be a spinster? "Does this have anything to do with Benjamin Hanson's sudden disappearance a few years ago?"

Amy shook her head, but her action lacked conviction to Emily's mind. Amy had sulked for months after the man's departure to serve in the Continental Army. Emily suspected Amy's heart underwent the same splitting in two her own had endured over Frank, yet she refused to admit such even to herself.

"What will Cousin Evelyn say?" Emily redirected the conversation away from the touchy subject.

"I believe my sister will understand and perhaps even applaud my choice. Her own marriage has not been, shall we say, what she expected." Amy cast a sideways glance at Emily. "Indeed, the abuse she suffers informs my desire as much as... Gramercy, it makes no difference now. I shall join you in your vow."

"Amy, my dear, surely you jest," Samantha said. "You'll break the heart of every bachelor in town."

"That is none of my affair, Samantha," Amy said, then chuckled. "After all, flirtation and marriage are very different activities."

Emily hugged her, the inner coil of tension relaxing as she grasped the fact she may not have to walk this path alone. "We need a nicer way to refer to ourselves than spinster, though, don't you think?"

"Definitely. But what?" Amy asked.

Emily tapped a finger against her chin, letting several possibilities run through her mind and discarding them as quickly. "A single man is called a bachelor, which is considered honorable." She wanted a positive word to refer to herself but could not think of any terms equivalent to spinster that didn't also carry a negative connotation. "William Shakespeare was known for creating new words; why not follow his lead?"

"He made up words?" Samantha set her tea down. "I was not aware."

"I'm amazed, my friend, that we found something you *didn't* know." Amy laughed. "Emily would. She's read everything he ever wrote."

"Bachelor girl?" Emily asked.

"That's a possibility," Amy said slowly. "Though I'm not sure about the girl part. We're a bit beyond girlhood, after all."

"True. How about bachelor-ette then?" Emily suggested. "The '-ette' addition makes it feminine."

Amy shook her head. "No, it sounds too funny. Perhaps we should avoid mentioning our desire to remain unwed and then we avoid the worry altogether."

Samantha glided to sit on a side chair, her shimmery green dress pooled around her, reflecting the flicker of flames in the fireplace. She leaned back in the chair, her right hand resting on her leg. "Am I correct in that you both wish to remain unwed? To forgo the pleasures of having a husband?"

Samantha's reference to the physical relations between husbands and wives in this setting surprised Emily for several reasons. She had not known her friend possessed such intimate knowledge of sexual relations. Indeed, having only become friends with Samantha the year before, surely there was much to discover about her past. Emily found herself practically holding her breath, waiting to hear what Amy prepared to say.

"Pleasures?" Amy leaned forward, one eyebrow lifted in question. "I cannot think of any pleasures associated with being married. From what little

I've heard, the event is short and no fun. At least not for the woman."

"It's not always weighted in the man's favor," Samantha said simply. "But are you both sure of this vow of remaining unmarried?"

"Without any doubt." Emily considered her friend for a long moment, realizing Samantha had adroitly changed the subject. Sadness shaded her friend's eyes, dimming their sparkle like clouds on a starry night.

"Yes, we shall be true unto ourselves," Amy added with a theatrical flourish of her hand, "and follow our heart's desires, rather than submit to the whimsical will of a man. Are you with us?"

Samantha contemplated the fire, dancing with red, orange, and blue licks of flame. Lost in thought, she lightly massaged the outside of her thigh. Shouts of laughter came through the window. A dog barked in response. Still, Samantha methodically caressed her leg with her fingers. Emily made a mental note to ask Samantha what had happened while she was visiting her grandmother in Savannah to cause the apparent ache in the limb. But that conversation could wait for another day. This was a momentous occasion in her life, and she wanted to savor it.

Samantha blinked and then regarded them. "I honestly never considered not marrying. The idea has its benefits, however."

Agitation mingled with hope forced Emily to her feet. She paced the room. When her father desired something, he didn't back down. He'd never give up until he had coerced her into the one act she longed to avoid. That was the problem. He wanted her to marry, and soon, for her protection, he said. She wouldn't put it past him to find her a husband despite her wishes. His demand coupled with her sister's recent death solidified the idea percolating in the back of her mind. The vacant shop wouldn't be vacant for long, no matter the obstacles placed in her way.

"So you are with us, Samantha?" Amy asked.

"Yes, but we must keep it between us, to avoid open scorn whenever possible." Samantha grinned. "After all, we've reached the upper end of marriageable age. We may as well."

Emily crossed to the center of the room, her hands outstretched. The first steps of a journey often proved the hardest. "Come, then, let us take a vow together to keep this choice our secret."

Amy and Samantha rose and clasped hands with Emily, forming a triangle of friendship.

"How binding is this vow?" Samantha asked. At the startled response from Amy and Emily, she added, "I mean, should one or the other of us change our minds, is that allowed as well?"

The image of Frank's blond good looks and

gray eyes floated before Emily. No matter how handsome and fine Frank or any man might be, the vow must, for her own peace of mind, be made. An inner voice cried out in anguish when she pushed the handsome face aside, locking it away in her heart. However, she did not want to force the restriction, or the pain, on anyone else. With a deep breath, Emily said, "As long as it is not coerced upon us, but is of our own choosing, I see no need for this to be forever binding."

"Then so be it," Samantha said. "I choose to remain unwed."

Amy cocked her head and smiled at Samantha. Squeezing her hand, she said, "But you have not stated your reason. What prompts you to this decision?"

A dour smile flickered across Samantha's lips. "Let us say, I have loved and lost and will not endure such pain again."

"Indeed?" Amy quirked an eyebrow at Samantha, then glanced at Emily.

Samantha bobbed her head once as a tiny smile formed on her lips. The woman contained many secrets, secrets Emily hoped to one day learn more about so she better understood her friend. For now, Emily's relief that her confidantes stood with her swept aside her earlier uncertainty.

Emily broke away from the triangle and poured three glasses of sweet sherry. "Then we shall celebrate our agreement with a toast." Handing the glasses around, she raised hers.

"What shall we toast to?" Samantha asked.

"To life, liberty and the pursuit of happiness for *all* in America." Emily flashed a smile at her comrades.

"And a more perfect union for women," Amy added, her eyes sober.

Emily tapped her glass against the others, happy yet fearing the consequences of their vow as the ring of crystal quivered into silence.

ABOUT THE AUTHOR

Betty Bolté writes both historical and contemporary stories featuring strong, loving women and brave, compassionate men. No matter whether the stories are set in the past or the present, she loves to include a touch of the paranormal. In addition to her romantic fiction, she's the author of several nonfiction books and earned a Master's in English in 2008. She is a member of Romance Writers of America, the Historical Novel Society, the Women's Fiction Writers Association, and the Authors Guild. Get to know her at www.bettybolte.com.

CPSIA information can be obtained
at www.ICGtesting.com
Printed in the USA
LVHW08s1724020718
582346LV00005B/35/P